KT-465-901

fic2

C015416587

SPECIAL MESSAGE TO READERS

THE ULVERSCROFT FOUNDATION
(registered UK charity number 264873)

was established in 1972 to provide funds for
research, diagnosis and treatment of eye diseases.
Examples of major projects funded by
the Ulverscroft Foundation are:-

- The Children's Eye Unit at Moorfields Eye
  Hospital, London
- The Ulverscroft Children's Eye Unit at Great
  Ormond Street Hospital for Sick Children
- Funding research into eye diseases and
  treatment at the Department of Ophthalmology,
  University of Leicester
- The Ulverscroft Vision Research Group,
  Institute of Child Health
- Twin operating theatres at the Western
  Ophthalmic Hospital, London
- The Chair of Ophthalmology at the Royal
  Australian College of Ophthalmologists

You can help further the work of the Foundation
by making a donation or leaving a legacy.
Every contribution is gratefully received. If you
would like to help support the Foundation or
require further information, please contact:

THE ULVERSCROFT FOUNDATION
The Green, Bradgate Road, Anstey
Leicester LE7 7FU, England
Tel: (0116) 236 4325

website: www.foundation.ulverscroft.com

TWILIGHT TRAIL

When manhunter Teel Barsom brings in notorious outlaw Slade Heath he makes a fateful mistake, destroying the new life he's built with his young bride and riddling his nightmares with guilt and loss. Trapped in a world of whiskey and shame, Teel wants nothing more than to sink into despair — then a mysterious young woman abducts him from the saloon and offers him redemption. But with salvation comes a price, one that may cost him and his kidnapper their lives . . .

LANCE HOWARD

TWILIGHT TRAIL

Complete and Unabridged

LINFORD
Leicester

First published in Great Britain in 2012 by
Robert Hale Limited
London

First Linford Edition
published 2014
by arrangement with
Robert Hale Limited
London

Copyright © 2011 by Lance Howard
All rights reserved

*A catalogue record for this book is available
from the British Library.*

ISBN 978–1–4448–1887–1

F	HAMPSHIRE COUNTY LIBRARY
	CO15416587
	9781444818871

This book is printed on acid-free paper

For Tannenbaum

Howard Lance Hopkins
December 12, 1961 — January 12, 2012

*'I read to escape . . . I write to help others
escape . . . '*

We all love and miss you:

*Dominique, Mom & Dad,
Robyn, Sam, Steap, Victor & Madeleine
All of your loving Family, Friends and
Loyal Readers*

1

The bright October sun blazed from a sky of chilled sapphire the day death rode into the Barsom ranch compound.

Three riders, dusters stippling, battered hats pulled low, slowed their mounts as they approached the outskirts of the ranch. Their faces scarred by the elements, and dead eyes pegging them as hardcases, the men were on a mission of destruction and retribution.

The front rider's gloved hand swept up, signaling the others to stop. Dark eyes peered across the grounds, which consisted of gentle rolling rises and grassy swales peppered with occasional stands of cottonwood and outbuildings — an icehouse, barn, shed — and an empty corral. The ranch was small as far as Texas spreads went, no more than a few hundred head of longhorn cattle, the mark of a man just starting out. The thought brought hesitation to the leader's mind, something buried deep within the man he might have been, a single compunction, making him wish he did not have to do the job he'd been sent to do. But the regret flickered, a candle in the wind. It was the woman or himself, for if he failed to complete the mission his days on this earth were indeed limited. Slade Heath brooked no disobedience, tolerated few mistakes.

Jep Wilson was a sonofabitch himself, and he knew it. Robbing banks, stages, and an occasional killing meant little to him, as long as he got what he wanted. And right now what he wanted was to go on living. That would not happen if Slade got out of the marshal's cell and found this mission unfinished. For as hard a man as Jep had become, Slade was harder.

A small clapboard ranch house squatted in the middle of the grounds, its sole chimney puffing white smoke. Wasn't far from supper time, Jep reckoned, and the woman, a newly wed, would be preparing vittles for that man of hers, Teel Barsom. A fool. A goddamn loco fool. Jep shook his head. Barsom should have known better than to accuse Slade of that killing and bring him in.

The ranch house looked so . . . tranquil under the October sun. Jep wondered what it would have been like if he'd owned his own ranch, never set out on the life he now led, never met up with Slade Heath. But, hell, scrounging for every dime and working his fingers to the bone wouldn't have suited him, anyhow. Taking what they wanted, needed, desired, was far easier. And why tie yourself to the love of one woman when you could have the comfort of many bar gals you never had to answer to? Fool. That's what Barsom was, indeed. A damned fool.

Yet in some small way, Jep envied him.

'Something wrong, Jep?' the blond-haired rider to his right asked, as he reined up. The man's name was Dickson, and if he had more than a spoonful of brains Jep would have been surprised. The owlhoot took orders without question, and was as lacking in compassion as he was in smarts. His nose was damn near flat from having been broken a handful of times and his brown eyes were bloodshot and dull.

'Just scanning the grounds.' Jep shifted in his saddle. The scents of coffee and baking beans now reached his nostrils, along with the musk of old leaves carried on the autumn breeze. Again, regret niggled at him. 'Don't want any surprises if Barsom ain't in town the way he's s'posed to be.'

Dickson laughed, somehow finding humor in the situation. The third man, Harris, reined up to Jep's left. Harris was a notch brighter than Dickson, but every bit as vicious. His long brown hair, straggling from beneath his hat rippled in the breeze and his jade eyes roved.

'Don't look that way to me.' Dickson eyed Jep with suspicion. 'You ain't goin' soft, are you? Looks like you're havin' second thoughts about this.'

Jep's right hand dropped to his waist, came back up in a blur, his Smith & Wesson aimed at the other man. 'You best bury that line of thinkin' or you'll be swallowin' lead.'

Dickson chuckled. 'You know I'm just joshin' you, Jep. None of us like havin' to kill a defenseless woman. That sonofabitch's own fault we got to do it.'

Dickson was lying. Jep heard it in his voice, saw it in the skull-like glint in his eyes. He would indeed enjoy this. He placed no value on human life, same as Slade, except Slade preferred to prolong the suffering when it suited him, enjoy it. That was why they were here. The woman inside would not suffer, but her husband . . . that was another matter.

Damn fool.

A fleeting regret made Jep wish that damned marshal in town just up and hanged Slade.

'Do it quickly, Dickson.' Jep lowered his gun, holstered it. 'Can't risk getting seen.'

Dickson nodded, drew his own gun, as did Harris.

It was time. No more delaying. With a spark of humanity, he wished this wasn't his life. But it was. The die had been cast a long time ago.

'Yah!' he yelled, slamming his heels into his mount's sides. The horse bolted forward.

The other two outlaws followed suit, spurring their horses towards the ranch house.

The sound of thunder filled the air and gray clouds of gunsmoke drifted across the compound like malevolent genies. Shots roared in Jep's ears, drowning out any whispers of regret that might have surfaced.

Glass exploded from windows under the hail of bullets hitting the house and splinters lacerated the air. The door started to open and he glimpsed a young woman with red hair. He quickly turned his head, and swore he heard a scream tear above the din of gunfire, but it might only have been an echo of his guilt. Whatever the case, no one came out of the house and he reckoned that was because no one was capable of doing so any longer. The woman who'd opened the door was now dead and perhaps that was a small consolation: it had been quick.

Now, the job was his. As he rode, his hand slipped into a saddle-bag, drew out a bottle half full of kerosene and stoppered with a rag. Reining up, his face tightening, he fished a match from his duster pocket. After striking it to light on a tooth, he touched the match to the rag. Flame reflecting in his eyes, he hurled the bottle at the porch that ran the length of the ranch house. The bottle shattered against the boards with an explosion and flames *whooshed* across the timber. Fire swept up the sides of the house, devouring shutters and walls, flashed across the porch boards. No screams came from within, and for that he was thankful.

The house went fast. Flames roared into the afternoon sky, engulfing every inch of the homestead. Great snapping pops and almost human-like whines filled the air. Beams groaned, creaked, crashed to the ground. It was as if the place were a living thing, a dying thing, gasping its last. But more than a simple structure perishing, Jep reckoned; it was the death of a man's dream, and that was exactly what Slade Heath wanted.

'Damn you, Slade,' Jep muttered, then reined around. He repeated the bottle procedure with the barn, icehouse and shed, setting them all aflame. Great plumes of black smoke billowed into the air and the whooping and incessant laughter of Dickson cascaded with the roar of flames. Jep had half a notion to put lead in the lowly bastard, might have if Harris hadn't been along, so he could have blamed it on someone shooting back from inside the house.

It was over in an eternity, or at least what felt like one to Jep. In reality, it took only fifteen minutes to level the buildings, then the three outlaws were riding away from the burning ruins of a man's life.

2

Teel Barsom was not an old man but at that moment he sure as hell felt as if he'd lived an entire lifetime in the past twenty-four hours.

In his twenty-six years he'd seen more than many men double his age, much of it not meant to be seen. The worst the West had to offer, in men and in deeds. And in the past few years he'd garnered himself quite a reputation as a manhunter, most of it due to hack writers looking to manufacture heroes in their dime novels — and damn near gettin' him buried by every greenhorn gunfighter hoping to notch out a reputation.

Shaking his head, he lifted his whiskey glass to his lips and let the amber liquid flow down his throat. It burned, set a fire in his belly, but still couldn't chase away the chill burrowed into his soul.

The Coopersville Saloon held few patrons at this time of the afternoon, but it wouldn't be long before cowhands from the local ranches started filtering in. At that moment, only one other man, far into his cups, sat hunched over a table nearby. Topaz sunlight streamed in a dust-sparkled arc through the large front window, and a bar girl stood at the end of the chipped bar that ran parallel to the north wall, leaning an elbow lazily upon it, a vacant expression on her coral-and kohl-painted face. She knew she had no mark in the man named Teel Barsom; no other woman but his Tessa did.

His gaze went to the gold band on his left ring finger and he could not help the smile that flickered across his lips, despite the gravity of the decision weighing on his mind.

Then reality crashed back in, settling over him like dark cloud.

A decision. One he should never have had to make. One he did not want to make. But one in which he had no choice.

'You should have never taken him in, you stupid bastard,' he told himself, voice heavy with regret.

They'd married only six months ago, and he'd promised her he would give up manhunting, start that little ranch they'd talked about the whole time they'd been courting. And he had. He'd said goodbye to his profession the moment he'd said 'I do' to her.

God, he loved that woman.

That was why he had no choice. No choice whatsoever.

It had been more accident than anything else, stumbling over Slade Heath killing that bank man's wife. Slade had either wanted information out of her, or had planned to kidnap her to use against the manager, as far as Teel could figure, but the outlaw had made a mistake in trying to hold up her buck-board just outside of town. Slade had caused the woman to panic, try to escape, and had shot at her to make her stop. The buckboard's horse had come up short, reared, and she'd been thrown

11

from the seat, hitting her head on a rock when she landed on the ground.

Teel had been on his way to town for supplies, had seen Slade fire the shot, cause the woman's death, otherwise the outlaw would have gotten away with it.

The irony of it was, Slade Heath was a man suspected of many crimes — murder, robbery, rape — but no one had ever been able to pin anything on him. He normally chose his marks carefully, never left witnesses. Teel, in his manhunting days, had nearly crossed paths with him a time or two, but the man always managed to avoid a noose or jail time.

Which was why Teel had brought him in, despite leaving manhunting behind. Though the outlaw was indirectly responsible for the woman's death, it was the first time anyone had a living witness to one of his crimes, the skill with a Peacemaker to bring him in, and the credibility to make a charge stick. Slade had proved a coward, the way most of his kind did, refusing to shoot it out with Teel. The man would not hang but Marshal Betts and the town council were aiming to see to it he spent a few years in jail.

But that would not happen, now, would it? Because last night one of Slade's men had made it entirely too plain to Teel that with any testifying came the death of his wife and the burning down of his ranch.

It used to be so easy before Tessa came into his life. Everything was so black and white. He went after men like Slade and brought them in or brought them down. Simple. But now he had something men such as Slade could use against him, and things were no longer simple at all. That was why he had given up that life for her. Only dumb luck and his damnable instinct for justice had interfered.

Slade was not like other outlaws or Teel would not have been sitting in this saloon, trying to drink away his conscience. He'd seen it immediately in the outlaw's eyes and felt it with that sixth sense man-hunters developed after countless nights on the trail. The man's eyes were empty of remorse or compassion, mercy or respect for life. If it had been anyone else, Teel would have shrugged off the threat as the bluster of a cornered outlaw. But not Slade. He meant what he said. He *would* kill Tessa.

Teel lifted his glass to his lips, swallowed another deep drink of the whiskey, draining the glass.

Damnit. Why had this choice been forced on him? If he marched over to the marshal's office and did what he had been told to do by Slade's man, Tessa would live . . . but the bank man's wife would not rest in peace and Teel's principles . . .

He flung the glass suddenly, fury sweeping through him. The glass hit a wall, shattered, and the barkeep and dove peered at him, shock sweeping across their faces. He couldn't blame them. They'd never seen him act in such a way, as long as he'd been coming here.

He ran a hand through his unkempt brown hair, sighed, then rose to his feet, the 'keep and girl still staring. For a moment, his gaze locked on his reflection between two hutches filled with liquor bottles in the big gilt-framed mirror behind the bar. He'd aged ten years since last night, he reckoned. His hazel-blue eyes were weary with the decision he was being forced to make. Tessa had seen it, too, in his eyes, on his face, in the tense set of his six-foot lanky frame. She had known something was wrong, but not what.

Judas Priest, what was he doing? If he let the outlaw walk free, it wasn't just the banker's wife who wouldn't rest in peace, not merely his own conscience that would forever be plagued with guilt. Slade was responsible for a spate of unproven crimes and each of those crimes had victims who deserved to see the man pay for what he had done.

But Tessa . . . he couldn't lose her, couldn't risk that Slade's man was bluffing, though he was certain that was not the case.

He didn't know how long he stood there, staring into the mirror, drowning in his own thoughts, but when his gaze focused the 'keep and girl were still staring at him, puzzled more than shocked, now. The lone patron was too drunk to care and paid him no mind.

It didn't matter. He was simply delaying the inevitable. The decision had been made the moment the man threatened his wife. Things were no longer black and white. They were scarlet.

He reached into his trouser pocket, drew out a roll of greenbacks and peeled off a couple. After tossing them on to the bar, he returned the rest to his pocket then gazed at the bartender.

'For the glass . . . ' he mumbled and the barman nodded, but remained silent. Both he and the dove watched Teel walk to the three steps leading to the small landing, pause, a shudder going through his body.

I can't do this . . .
You have to!

He took the three steps like a bull being dragged into a slaughterhouse, then pushed through the batwings into the afternoon sunlight.

The air carried a chill and he shuddered again, but it wasn't from the cold. It was from the loathsome duty he was about to perform. What kind of man gave in to threats, let an outlaw dictate his actions?

A man who loved his wife more than life itself.

A defeated man. A man with no choice.

The walk to the marshal's office was like the carrying of a coffin to the bone-yard. Every step was a burden, his feet lead, his heart bleeding stone.

He could not imagine what Marshal Betts was going to think, the shame with which the lawman would look upon him every day for the rest of his life. What would Tessa think when she found out, for that matter? Would she forgive him? Would she still look upon him as the man she'd married?

God help me . . .

When he reached the marshal's office he placed a trembling hand on the doorhandle, stood frozen, gripping it so tightly his fingers drained bone white.

Please don't make me do this . . .

Begging to an unseen God was not going to help. The choice was his alone, forced upon him. No avenging lightning from Heaven would strike Slade dead and save him from the task.

Forcing himself to move, he twisted the handle, stepped inside, and shut the door behind him. Marshal Betts, an older man with iron side-whiskers and wisps of gray hair on a balding pate, looked up from where he was seated behind his desk as Teel entered.

'Well, Teel, pleasure to see you, my boy!' A grin spread across the lawman's face. 'What brings you in?'

Belly plunging, Teel gave the lawman a short nod, then shifted his gaze to the bank of three cells at the back of the office. A man sat on the edge of the bunk in the center cell, head down, locks of twisted brown hair falling around his face. The very sight of Slade Heath sent a knife of guilt through Teel's heart and a shiver of dread through his nerves, and he knew — *knew* — he was wrong in coming here, doing what he was about to do, but it wouldn't change a thing.

The man's head lifted, cold gray eyes coming to bear on Teel. Heath's eyes were utterly lifeless, as dead as the first time Teel had looked into them. A scar ran from one corner of his mouth to his left ear and if ever there had been a more merciless face on God's Green, Teel had not seen it. The man was a monster.

A ghost of a grin flickered over Slade's face and Teel forced his gaze away.

'I've . . . ' he said, voice hitching, as he looked back to the marshal. 'I've come to confess I've made a mistake.'

'What?' The marshal rose from his

chair, puzzlement locking on his round ruddy features. 'What kind of mistake, Teel? Something wrong with Tessa? You look white as a ghost.'

'No, nothing with Tessa.' He shook his head, swallowed. 'You got the wrong man in that cell, Marshal. It wasn't him who caused that woman's death.'

'What the hell you mean it wasn't him?' Shock replaced perplexity on the lawdog's face. 'What are you talking about, Teel? What do you mean it wasn't Slade?'

'I lied, Marshal. I knew that man Slade was a suspect in a passel of crimes, so I said it was him.' He had rehearsed the story a dozen times in his mind since last night, but it still came out sounding as fake as the first time he'd tried it on, and the marshal, by his expression, didn't believe a word of it.

'That's goddamn nonsense, Teel. I know you better than that. You ain't a liar.'

Teel glanced at Slade, who was smiling a cold smile. 'Afraid I am, Marshal. I just wanted to help.'

The marshal scratched his head, glanced at Slade, then back to Teel. Suspicion crawled into the man's eyes.

'If there's a reason you're afraid of him, Teel, I'll deputize some men, see to it you and Tessa are protected.'

That would have made it so simple, wouldn't it? If he could just accept that offer. But a look at the man in the cell told him nothing under God's Heaven the marshal could do would protect them from Slade Heath's wrath.

'You don't goddamn know me at all, Marshal! I don't need your help.' He put anger into his voice to cover his guilt, which wasn't difficult, considering the fury he felt for the man in that cell, but he could tell Betts still didn't believe him.

'What are you sayin', Teel?' The law-man's eyes hardened, drilled into him.

'That you got the wrong man and I won't testify against him.'

'I'd have to let him go. You were the only witness.'

'I know. But I won't stand against him.

21

He wasn't responsible for that woman's death.'

The marshal shook his head, frowned. 'Even if you change your mind, you won't have a lick of credibility anymore. You're willing to throw away a chance to put this man away for a few years?'

'I . . . have no choice.' His voice lowered, laden with guilt.

'You do have a choice, Teel. Don't do this. You were a hell of a manhunter.'

'Those days are gone. I got a wife, now. She comes first.'

'Teel — '

'You got the wrong man, Marshal. I won't testify. That's all there is to it.'

'You're sure you want to do this?' A plea came in the marshal's tone. If there were any chance of changing his mind, the time was now. Another word and the decision was irreversible.

'I am. Let him go.' Something died inside him with those words and the reflection of disappointment and disgust on the lawman's face put the nails in the coffin.

The marshal sighed, and his shoulders slumped. He went to a key ring hanging on a wall peg, lifted it off slowly, as if hoping Teel would stop him before he opened that cell.

But he couldn't. Wouldn't.

The lawdog went to the cell, unlocked the door and swung it open. 'You're free to go.'

Slade came to his feet, walked slowly to the cell door. 'Thanks for your hospitality, Marshal. And the fine vittles from the café. Reckon I never got such homey treatment before.' The outlaw laughed a low laugh, then brushed past the marshal, whose features appeared utterly defeated.

Slade stopped beside Teel and Teel felt the urge to recoil but held his ground.

'You stay the hell away from my wife,' Teel said in a voice low enough not to carry to the marshal.

Slade's cold gray eyes locked with his. 'You made the right choice this time, Barsom . . . but you never should have taken me in in the first place. You might say it burns me up.' The outlaw grinned, the threat plain. 'We'll be seein' each other again, I reckon. Least . . . I'll be seein' you.'

Slade stepped past Teel and opened the door, then with a final glance back at Teel and the marshal, closed it behind him as he left.

A chilled wave washed over Teel. He peered at the floor, unable to meet the lawman's gaze.

'What have you done, Teel?' the lawdog said, going back to his desk and tossing the keys atop some papers scattered there.

'What I had to do, Marshal. What I had to do.'

3

Teel Barsom had known it would be hard going against his very nature, but it was worse than he thought. It felt as if everything inside of him had withered, save one emotion — his love for Tessa. If she weren't waiting for him, he doubted he could live with himself. He prayed he wouldn't see the same disgust in her eyes as he had seen in the marshal's. But he had done what needed doing to save her and that was that. What other men thought of him, what he thought of himself, made no difference. When it came time for his judgment he could only hope the Lord above took pity on him for caring more about the woman waiting on him back at the ranch than himself.

He rode the short trail leading out of town at a dirge pace, mustering the courage he would need when he faced her. He would have to tell her what he'd done. There was no way around it. He'd never lied to her and he wasn't about to start now. There had been enough lies this day.

A strange dread suddenly crawled up from inside him and Slade's god-ugly face flashed into his mind. It was that same sixth sense manhunters felt on the trail, though for the life of him he didn't know why he felt it, now. It was a bit late, wasn't it? Damage was done.

He shook it off, the chilly late autumn air brisk against his face as he rode. Variegated leaves on stands of oak and aspen to either side of the trail shivered with the hush of the breeze.

You let a monster loose on this town . . .

Guilt shuddered through his being, not for the first time and not for the last. What would Slade do now? Surely he knew the marshal would be keeping a closer eye on him. But would that matter? From experience, he knew outlaws were a cocky lot. To present, though accused of many, Slade had never been convicted of a crime. As much as Teel wished the man would move on, make some kind of mistake that would get him a necktie party, he couldn't count on such.

That meant innocent folks would get hurt and Teel would bear the burden for each and every one of them.

His hands tightened on the reins and he forced away a knot of emotion choking his throat. He wished he could go back in time, avoid the day he'd ever thought of becoming a manhunter, and the day he'd stumbled across Slade Heath.

But that was as impossible as disposing of the shame he now bore.

A scent caught his attention, pulling him from his thoughts. Smoky, acrid, not the pleasant musk of a chimney or camp-fire, woodsy yet scorched, and for an unknown reason he shivered. Dread returned, stronger, poisoning his veins and sizzling in his nerves.

Something is wrong . . .

Without consciously implementing

the action, he slapped his heels into his mount's sides, driving the big bay into a faster gait along the trail. His gaze lifted above the fall-pigmented tops of the now-thinning trees, focusing on a plume of black smoke drifting through the sky. The smoke was like some great nebulous bird of dark portent, shape ever-changing, dispersing like the integrity he had set adrift within himself this day.

'No . . . ' The word came from his lips unbidden, as black as that smoke. His hands tightened on the reins, making his hands and forearms ache.

The woods gave way to grassy rolling rises and dipping swales. The odor of singed wood grew heavier, assailing his senses, and images flashed into his mind; Tessa's face, smiling, laughing, her lips whispering, 'I love you,' then saying 'goodbye'.

'Noo!' His voice snapped like a whip, now, and he drove the mount harder.

He knew. He knew with everything they had together and everything he was: she was gone. A great gaping emptiness opened inside of him with the thought, a forever hole.

Another thought struck him: all he had thrown away this day had been for nothing.

The trail melded into grassland and his heart pounded with growing panic. The horse's hoofs beat the ground, swallowing yards, and he struggled to hold on to his composure. Just a few more minutes . . . just a few more —

'No! Oh, Jesus, no!' he screamed as the compound came into view.

What was left of it. For all that remained were devils of black smoke and memories never made. The outbuildings, the barn, the house were all gone, now just smoldering shards of wood that looked like black bones. Dead dreams, all of it.

Because, it became horribly clear, he now knew what Slade Heath had meant when he said Teel should never have taken him in in the first place. He had trusted the word of an outlaw, a word that meant nothing.

'You bastard!' he yelled, jerking the reins and bringing the bay to a halt as he neared the remains of the house.

He leaped from the saddle, ran towards the blackened ruins, his legs trembling, nearly sending him pitching to the ground.

Snapping bursts of flame occasionally came from the charred beams as he stormed into the debris. Smoke stung his eyes and heat singed the hairs on his forearms and brows.

'Tessa!' he yelled, knowing it was useless. 'Oh, God, please, no. Tessa!' He stumbled in the debris, fell, hands grasping a burnt beam, pain immediately blistering across his palms. He gasped, tears streaming down his face, dripping on to the blackened beam, sizzling, turning to steam.

Hands burning, he grabbed the beam again, hurled it aside, ignoring the pain, in some desperate hope he would find nothing beneath, that somehow . . . somehow his new life wasn't over.

A moment later, that ember of fragile hope flickered out. For beneath a beam that had once been part of the front doorway, he glimpsed a soot-blackened wedding ring.

4

Eleven months later

Hunched over a table at the Coopersville Saloon, Teel Barsom took another swig from the bottle of rotgut whiskey sitting in front of him. The liquor burned, but he'd long ago ceased to notice or care. He slammed the bottle down, whiskey dripping from one corner of his mouth, trickling over his chin. The room spun before his vision, the early evening crowd streaking into a blurred mélange of colors. Sounds swelled around him, the giggling from bar girls and whoops of men winning at Faro or chuck-a-luck; the curses from cowboys losing at poker. A tinkler banged discordant notes that jangled with the other noises hammering at his brain.

Every night the same. More whiskey, more guilt. The money he'd built up in the bank from his years of manhunting had just about run out, but he didn't give a damn about that, either. He didn't give a damn about anything.

Because the nightmare was still the same, and still came each night the moment he fell asleep. Unless he could get drunk enough to pass out and wallow in merciful blackness.

A groan escaped his lips as the scene of the fire-gutted ranch house flashed through his memory. Despite the alcoholic haze gripping his senses, the pain still stung as acutely, as freshly, as if it had occurred yesterday. He prayed for it to end, but it never did. No God heard his plea or gave a damn. Perhaps this was his lot, to suffer, and perhaps he deserved it for what he had done.

His trembling fingers went to a pocket in his denim shirt, pulled out a gold band, one that matched the one that had once encircled his left ring finger. He'd buried that one with her remains. He stared through blurry vision at the smudged band, tears welling but not falling. He'd taken it off her body, the only thing of hers, save memories, he had left.

Before his mind rose her face, framed in soft red curls, her doe-blue eyes smiling, the way they had on the day they wed. Then her face became a blackened skull, grinning, and he pressed his eyes shut against the image, trying to force it away. At last it vanished and he opened them again, the room now jittering instead of spinning.

He tucked the ring back into his pocket, grabbed the bottle and took another swig. It took more of the liquor, now, for him to reach a place where he could not feel the pain, the guilt. No, that wasn't quite right: a place where he could tolerate it, if only for a few hours.

Christamighty, he missed that woman.

It was his fault she was gone. He'd made a damned fool decision the day he'd brought in Slade Heath and an even poorer one the day he'd helped set him free. Fate had gotten even with him that day, and had not stopped twisting the knife since.

Slade Heath had gone nowhere. Fact, he'd been more brazen, more mocking, he and his men walking the town freely, no crimes pinned on them to stop them from doing so, though robberies of stages coming into the surrounding towns had continued unabated. No witnesses were ever left behind and no proof led to Slade Heath, and that was Teel's fault, too. He'd signed so many death certificates in aiding Slade's release, he might as well have pulled the trigger himself.

Slade Heath and his three men had taken up rooms at the hotel, often came into the saloon at night to engage the saloon girls. They mocked him with their gazes, their knowing laughs.

He wanted to kill them, gun them down where they stood, but he had never been a cold-blooded killer and his skills had eroded with months of drink; he would lose if he drew on Slade.

Perhaps that would be best, he often thought. Death would end the pain, the guilt, and the Devil had a room all ready for him. But some spark of something kept him from doing it. Tessa would not want him to go out that way, though she damn well wouldn't have liked to see what had become of him, the pathetic excuse of a man he was now.

And if he shot Slade dead, by some peculiar irony of Fate, Teel would be the one who went to the gallows. With no evidence against the outlaw, in the eyes of the law he would have murdered an 'innocent' man. He couldn't prove Slade had killed Tessa and burned the ranch to the ground; hell, he had the perfect alibi: he'd been standing right next to Teel when it happened.

But he *was* responsible. Of that, Teel had no doubt. Yet there was no way to make him pay, and as much as Teel had rehearsed it in his mind, he was no killer. He had shot men in self-defense, buried a few to protect his own life or that of another, but there was a difference between that and simply walking up to a man and putting a bullet in him.

His gaze lifted, blurred vision focusing on the barroom. Cowboys and bar gals ignored him, had learned long ago he was nothing more than a drunk now, a man who used to be. His reputation was gone, along with his integrity. For a spell, they had peered at him with disgust, shame, knowing what he had done and that because of him Slade Heath walked about their town without restraint. They blamed him, as well as the outlaws, for every bank or stage robbed, every innocent person killed.

The marshal had tried talking to him a few times early on, but Teel had proved inconsolable, then downright belligerent. At last, folks just left him alone.

Another gulp of the whiskey. His belly roiled, and nausea sent bile burning into his throat. His body wasn't going to hold up to much more of the abuse he was putting it through. And that was just fine, in his estimation. He was no good to anybody, or to himself.

'If pity were gold,' he mumbled, holding up the whiskey bottle and peering into the amber liquid. 'You'd be a king, wouldn't you, Teel?' But pity was all he had left.

Through the liquid, distortedly, he saw the batwings open and two men step into the saloon. They stood, poised, on the short landing. Teel thumped down the bottle, a burst of impotent rage sizzling through his nerves.

Two of Slade's men, the ones called Dickson and Harris, stood looking over the barroom. Some of the noise quieted the moment they stepped in and two of the bar girls scurried for the stairs at the back of the saloon that led to the upstairs rooms where the doves plied their trade. They wanted no part of Slade's boys, though as Teel knew from experience that wouldn't make a lick of difference. A number of cowboys cast them looks but would do nothing against them. Maybe that didn't make them a hell of a lot less cowardly than himself.

The one named Dickson grinned, slapped Harris on the shoulder and pointed towards Teel. Harris gave Dickson a vacant grin, then both came down the three steps leading to the barroom proper.

They navigated their way to the bar, signaled a bottle from the barkeep, who appeared none too pleased to serve them.

Teel's belly sank as the men then headed in his direction.

Dickson pulled out a chair to Teel's right and seated himself. Harris took one to the left, sat. Dickson uncapped the bottle, took a swig, though he appeared as if he'd started drinking long before he came into the bar.

'Get the hell away from me,' Teel said, eyeing Dickson. The outlaw's face shimmered before his vision.

'Why, what kind of a welcome is that, Barsom?' Dickson set the bottle down, slid it across to Harris, who grabbed it and raised it to his lips. 'You ain't bein' friendly a-tall.'

'I don't aim to be. Don't want no part of you. Leave me be.'

Harris, setting the bottle down, laughed. 'I do believe Barsom don't like us, Dickson.'

Dickson nodded. 'I reckon you're right, Harris. Wonder if it's because of the way

I made his wife scream right before I blowed her brains out. Think that could be it, Harris?' Dickson let out a loud laugh.

Fury tore through Teel's veins. The son-ofabitch was admitting it but it wouldn't matter, because no one would take the word of a drunk, now, and even if they did, the hardcase would just deny he'd ever said it.

'You bastard!' Teel sprang to his feet, immediately wavering as the room spun. His hand went out, gripped the edge of the table to keep from falling.

Laughter hammered in his ears as his gaze struggled to focus.

Dickson had come out of his own seat, stood directly in front of Teel. Harris rose as well, getting behind him.

'Anytime you think you got the balls,' Dickson said, tone goading.

Teel wanted to draw on him, then, but he'd left his gun where he bedded down at night and was unarmed. He doubted he could have drawn even had he been heeled. He could barely stand.

'Your time's comin',' Teel muttered,

struggling to hold down his belly.

'That so, Barsom?' Dickson glanced at Harris, a vicious glint in his eye. 'I reckon this stupid drunk just threatened me, Harris. What do you think?'

'I heard it plain, Dickson. He shorely did.'

'Even Slade would understand I couldn't just let that pass.' Dickson's hands, palms flat, slammed into Teel's chest, and Teel went backwards. He would have gone down had Harris not thrust both his own hands against Teel's back and shoved him forward again.

Instinctively, Teel swung on Dickson, or at least tried to. His arm refused to work right. He got it halfway up, but Dickson pushed him backwards again. This time Harris grabbed both of Teel's arms and pinned them at his side.

Dickson buried a fist in Teel's belly, then followed up with a left cross to the jaw.

The room whirled again, blinked to black, then came back. Teel's legs buckled and he went down, hitting the floor on his side. Sawdust rose in a plume, settled over him.

'Next time you decide to threaten me, Barsom, you best be ready to back it up or I'll kill you. I don't care what Slade says.'

Dazed, Teel looked up, Dickson's features were blurry. He spat a stream of saliva and blood on to the outlaw's boot.

Dickson's face washed crimson, then he laughed and grabbed Teel's half-empty bottle of whiskey from the table.

'You're just a pathetic drunk, man-hunter. Hero to no one. Couldn't save your woman and can't save yourself.' Dickson tipped the bottle, poured a stream of rotgut on to Teel's head until the bottle was empty.

'You bastard,' Teel muttered, trying to push himself up.

Dickson drew back his foot, preparatory to kicking him in the face.

'That's enough!' a voice came from in front of the batwings.

Teel struggled to focus on two figures

standing just inside the doors, a man and a woman.

'Just funnin' him a bit, Marshal,' Dickson said, setting the bottle on the table. 'Was just about to help the poor drunk up.'

Harris chuckled, grabbed his own whiskey bottle from the table.

Marshal Betts came down the three steps to the barroom proper, followed by the person who had come in with him, a woman with hair the color of fresh raspberries and skin as white as alabaster, a splash of freckles across her pert nose. She was dressed in a blue blouse and riding skirt with buckshot sewn into the hem, and a flat hat that hung at her back. Teel had never seen her before and could barely see her now.

'Get out, both of you,' Marshal Betts said. A number of cowboys and the few bar girls still in the room stared at the proceedings. The barkeep came around the bar.

Dickson eyed the marshal with a look

that said he was a hair's breadth from drawing. But he apparently thought better of it, because a slow grin spread across his lips and he slapped Harris on the shoulder.

'Reckon I've had enough of this town's hospitality for the night, anyhow,' Dickson said, then stepped around Teel and headed for the batwings, Harris at his heels.

'We don't allow your kind of woman in here,' the 'keep said to the girl who'd come in with the marshal.

She turned to him, smiled. 'From the looks of what you do allow in here, I don't see where I'm a problem.'

The 'keep's face reddened, and it was obvious he was looking to take out his frustration with the situation on someone who wouldn't put a bullet in him.

As if by magic, a derringer appeared in the girl's hand and she straight-armed it at the bartender.

'Still got objections?' she asked, gaze locking with his.

His eyes narrowed and muscles balled to either side of his jaw. At last he shook his head. ' 'S'awright this time,' he mumbled.

'Paige.' The marshal shook his head.

The young woman smirked and pocketed the derringer in her skirt. 'Didn't have time for arguin'.' She stepped over to Teel, knelt, bracing one forearm across her skirt-covered knee. She peered at him, her blue eyes searching. He struggled to focus on her face.

'My name's Paige Hanner, Barsom. I'm here to redeem you.'

He thought for a moment he had heard her wrong, or that she was joking, but her tone told him she was entirely serious.

'I don't need redemption,' he said, wanting no part of whatever she was up to.

She chuckled, brushed sawdust off his shirt. 'I don't aim to give you a choice.'

She grabbed his arm, pulled as she rose to her feet. The marshal got on the other side, taking Teel's right arm and between him and the girl they hoisted Teel to unsteady feet.

They jammed their arms beneath his, half-dragged, half-walked him towards the batwings. Getting him up the three steps to the landing proved to be an exercise, but at last they pulled him out on to the boardwalk.

His belly suddenly objected to the case of the spins that gripped his mind and he stumbled forward, doubled over the rail and vomited on to the hard-pack of the street.

'Appreciate it if you got that out of your system now, Mr Barsom,' the girl said from behind him. 'Don't need you doin' it in the buckboard on the way back to my cabin.'

'I ain't goin' anywhere with you,' he managed to get out between retching.

'You'll go with her or spend the night in one of my cells, Teel,' the marshal said.

Teel was about to tell them both to go to hell when blackness began

46

sweeping in from the corners of his mind. He was barely conscious of them grabbing him before he hit the board-walk face first, then nothing more.

5

Morning sunlight arced through the parlor's front windows and stung like hell as Teel Barsom tried to pry open his eyelids. He quickly pressed them shut again against the glare, but even with his lids closed the brightness still stabbed into his brain like icepicks.

Someone was pounding on drums in his skull. Loud. His head felt ready to crack open and every little sound — the roar of blood throbbing through the small veins at his temples, a morning bird cheeping an ungodly racket somewhere beyond the windows — caused a ringing pain that was akin to getting hit in the teeth with a hammer.

He tried to lift his head from the pillow — at least he assumed it was a pillow, though it felt like soft stone — but any motion brought a corresponding and disproportionate agony inside his brain.

It was, unfortunately, a feeling with which he was well familiar.

He lay there, wherever there was, for he dared not try to open his eyes for the moment to find out, endeavoring to take deep breaths, which in reality were terribly shallow ones, because even that slightest movement caused further discomfort.

What the hell had happened? Damnit, it hurt even to think, but he forced himself to grasp at memories that came in a distorted jumble. The barroom. That was easy enough to recall, because that's where he spent every evening before staggering back to where he bedded down. Where he bedded down . . . from the feel of the pillow beneath his head he was certain he was not where he usually passed out.

A fight of some kind? Yes, two of Slade Heath's men had come in. One had hit him. Then, a woman . . .

A woman? He recalled a redhead, and she and the marshal had dragged him out of the saloon. Beyond that, he recollected nothing.

'I know you're awake, Mr Barsom,' a female voice came, followed by a loud clank that rang through his mind like a gunshot.

His eyelids flicked open and he let out a sharp gasp as sunlight again drove the twin icepicks into his brain.

'Judas Priest, woman,' he muttered, pressing his eyes closed again.

'Get up, Mr Barsom,' she said. 'Breakfast and chores are waitin'.'

Was she serious? Christ on a crutch, he hoped not. Something kicked his leg and he held the solid suspicion it was the woman standing over him. The same woman who'd pulled him out of the saloon last night.

He forced his eyes open, this time the glare causing slightly less agony.

'Why the hell did you kick me?' he asked, mouth feeling as if it were stuffed full of cotton and lips parched and cracked.

'You needed motivation getting up,

feeling like I'm guessing you feel, so I gave it to you. Reckon a little kick ain't about to pain you half as bad as your head does.'

She had that much right, because right now a shotgun blast to his skull would have pained him less.

'Who the hell are you?' He got his eyes to focus on her, at least in intervals. She was dressed in a denim shirt and riding skirt that did little to hide her generous figure, and had pulled her raspberry curls back into a tight bun. Her hands rested on her full hips and her blue eyes were narrowed and promising business.

'I told you last night, though I don't reckon you were in much condition to hold on to the information. My name's Paige Hanner.'

He tried to sit up, the room spinning as he did so. Nausea welled in his belly.

'If you're fixin' to hurl your innards again, don't do it in my parlor, Mr Barsom.'

'You're all sympathy,' he said, at last

achieving a sitting position.

'You don't need sympathy right now,' she said, folding her arms across her ample bosom. 'You've been pityin' yourself for so long, it would only do you an injustice.'

Her words sent a surge of anger through his veins, but it quickly ebbed, because she was right. He'd made self-pity an art form, but he didn't give a damn.

A glance told him he was sitting on a couch in the parlor of what looked to be a small cabin. The couch sat in the middle of the room, a few feet from a fireplace, above which rested a Winchester on wall pegs. A sideboard and hutch flanked the south wall, and a small kitchen adjoined the north. A closed door on the west wall led to what he assumed was a bedroom. Frost still coated the windows, so the hour was early; the frost was just starting to melt and ran in snaking rivulets down the panes.

Before him stood a small coffee table

holding a silver tray with biscuits and a blue enameled coffee pot. The thought of food brought a surge in the nausea and he struggled to force it away. Breakfast was not what he wanted or needed. What he wanted and needed was a horn of the bull that had gored him last night. It was the way he started every morning.

He tried to stand, fell right back to the couch. The crashing drums in his skull thundered up a handful of notches and the room gyrated.

'You should eat and have some coffee before attempting to stand, Mr Barsom.' She gave him an annoying little smile, looking for all the world like she was enjoying his misery.

'I don't want to eat,' he said, anger whipping in his tone. He pushed himself forward, came to his feet again, this time staying up. Muscles quivered in his legs, which threatened to buckle. The spinning of the room robbed him of balance, and his head hammered tenfold. Forcing a deep breath, nearly losing his stomach contents, he steadied, managed to get the room to slow to a stop a moment later.

The woman kept that damnable smile on her lips and it irritated the hell out of him. She watched him like a child watching a puppy running into furniture.

Another moment passed. He turned, kept his balance, then went to the sideboard and hutch and began opening doors and drawers.

'What are you looking for, Mr Barsom?' Paige asked, the grin remaining.

'Whiskey. You got any in this place?'

A small laugh came from her. 'I do.'

'Where the hell is it?'

'Where you can't get at it. In a storage space in the barn floor, but it's padlocked, so the information won't do you any good.'

He stared at her as if she had two heads. What was wrong with this woman? 'Why do you have it in there?'

'Because whiskey will do you as

much good as sympathy right now.'

It suddenly dawned on him his bare feet were touching cool floorboards and he gazed down to see he was wearing only the bottom part of his long underwear.

'Where are my clothes and who took me out of them?'

'On the chair in the kitchen and I did.'

'You took off my clothes?'

'Doubt you got anything I haven't seen before, Mr Barsom, and you're still wearing your bottoms, so quit your bellyachin'.'

He went to the kitchen, which was small and unearthly bright in his present state. It held only a table and a few chairs, and a trapdoor in the floor led to a root cellar. Yellow, flowered curtains dressed the window over the sink and a row of pans hung above the counter. Squinting, he located his clothes on a chair and pulled them on, checking to make sure Tessa's ring was still in his shirt pocket. At least the woman wasn't a thief.

Finished dressing, he returned to the parlor. Paige hadn't moved and her gaze stuck to him like a school marm's to an unruly child.

'Eat, Mr Barsom.' She nudged her chin at the tray of biscuits on the table.

Anger surged through his veins again for no reason he could really pinpoint. 'I told you I don't want your god-damned breakfast!' He went to the table, kicked it over. The tray made a clang as it hit the floor that rang through his skull and he instantly regretted the move. The blue enameled pot splashed coffee across the floor and small area rug. Biscuits rolled.

'Feel better?' Paige asked, appearing unmoved by his childish action.

'Who the hell are you? What do you want from me? What gives you the right to kidnap me and bring me here, wherever here is?'

The smile got wider. It pissed him off. He wasn't used to this type of treatment and it brought a memory to mind. Tessa sometimes had handled his bad moods in the same manner.

'I'm Paige,' she said, as if that told him all he needed to know.

'I already knew as much. That just tells me your name, not who you are.'

'That's all you need to know for the moment. As for the rest, you're in a cabin the marshal was kind enough to rent for me while I stay here in Coopersville for a spell. I did not kidnap you, as you so put it. I asked you if you wanted to come and since you were passed out in my buckboard at the time you gave me no objection.'

'Why am I here?' He was finding it difficult to get a handle on his thoughts through the pounding in his head and the confusion brought on by the after effects of that swill the 'keep served him.

'Told you last night. Redemption.'

'Why? What interest is it of yours whether or not I'm redeemed?'

'I will tell you that at the proper time, too, Mr Barsom. For now we have a journey and you set foot on the trail last night.'

'You're crazy.' He shook his head, realizing immediately it was a mistake as the room started to spin again. He managed to get it settled more quickly this time and some of the cotton was out of his mouth.

'That's entirely possible.'

'What do you want?'

'Like I said, in the proper time. Right now, however, what I want is wood chopped for the fire. Nights are getting colder and I don't know how long I am going to be staying here.'

'You expect me to chop wood for you?' Under other circumstances he would have thought the woman was having a joke at his expense, but her face told him she was entirely serious.

'I do.'

'You're kidding.'

'I'm not. In return for a place to sleep, food and your redemption, you will do chores, such as wood chopping. It will help cleanse the whiskey out of your system.'

He stared at her. She *was* serious.

And plumb loco. 'I didn't ask you for a place to sleep, food, or redemption.'

She shrugged. 'No, you did not.'

'I don't want them.'

'Yes, you do. You just don't know it yet.'

He wasn't sure what to say. Somehow he'd ended up hung over in the house of a crazy woman and Marshal Betts had helped. What the hell was going on?

'You honestly expect me to chop wood and dry out, all the while not telling me who you are and why the hell you want me redeemed?'

That irritating smile came back to her lips. 'That's the way I see it. The wood and the ax are on the left side of the house. You best get started.' She paused. 'Oh, and I will expect you to eat the vittles I prepare for you from now on, instead of throwing them on the floor.'

'You're plumb loco.'

'You said that already. Don't change the facts any.' After righting the table, she went to the tray and coffee pot and picked them up, set them atop the table, then began picking up biscuits. He watched her, mouth agape, for one of the few times in his life at a loss for words. Before he could stop himself, he found he was standing outside on the porch, staring out at the gently rolling grasslands. He judged he wasn't far from town. There were a number of cabins in the area, some occupied, some not. This one came with a small barn and corral, which was empty, and a surrounding fence. The scent of browning grass haunted the air, and he couldn't recall the last time he had taken notice of such. He couldn't recollect the last time he'd started the day sober, either. He didn't care for the feeling a lick.

The day was brightening, and the sun had climbed a notch higher. He went down the stairs and around a small garden holding winter squash and pumpkin. Didn't she say the marshal had rented the place for her? Why was the garden tended and growing vegetables that took a while to mature?

Something about her story didn't ring true.

Paige Hanner, he thought, as he went around to the left side of the house. The name meant nothing to him. Why would a woman he'd never met bring him here with some peculiar intent to sober him up? And why was Betts involved?

His headache had receded only a fraction, but it still made him sorry he was not drinking his breakfast. He spotted an ax wedged in a stump and unsplit logs piled next to the house. A pair of heavy gloves lay next to the ax. He pulled them on, then yanked the ax free, if for no other reason than to siphon off some of the anger he felt at the woman for doing whatever the hell it was she was doing to him. He set a log on the stump, heaved the ax overhead and brought it down.

Missed. Judas Priest, he couldn't recollect the last time he'd done manual labor. He yanked the ax out of the stump, hoisted it above his head again. This time he hit the log, but it flew off the stump, unsplit.

Christ on a crutch, what the devil was he doing? Why was he even trying to do what she had told him to do? He didn't want any damned redemption. He wanted to bask in his own pity, because being sober meant he felt the pain and grief much more acutely.

Tessa. She was gone, would always be gone. And this woman was forcing him to be sober and do her chores.

And worst of all, he was doing it!

'The hell with this!' he muttered and buried the ax in the stump. He glared at the barn. Surely she had a horse in there, the one that must have pulled the buckboard she'd brought him here in. She couldn't keep him here if he didn't want to stay and that was that. And that damned marshal would get an earful about it, too.

He went towards the barn, anger driving away some of the banging in his skull. He wasn't sure whether he was more pissed off at her for presuming to pull him out of his wallow or at himself for actually starting to go along with it.

Reaching the barn, he stepped inside. It held only a trio of stalls; a bay in one and a pinto in another. The third was empty. He noted the padlocked trap-door in the floor just to the right of the doors. No time to try breaking it, and the noise would attract her. He certainly could not go back into the house for the key, either. No matter. He would pay the saloon a visit when he got to town. They opened for breakfast and the 'keep was used to him drinking his.

He went to the bay's stall. It was a fine horse, and he could send it back to her after he made his escape. He turned to look for a saddle, stopped short.

'Goin' somewhere, Mr Barsom?' Paige said from the entrance.

Damn. 'You can't keep me here. I don't know who the hell you really are or what you want, but I'm takin' this horse and ridin' the hell out of here. I'll send the horse back when I get to town, case you got any notion of reporting me as a horse thief.'

She peered at him, no smile, now. She appeared to be debating something, though he had no idea what it might be.

'Stay, Mr Barsom. I'm askin' you — please.'

His brow furrowed and his hazel-blue eyes narrowed. 'Why would I do that after the way you got me here, Miss Hanner, or whoever you really are.'

'Would you have come if I had just walked up to you and asked?'

'No.'

'There's your answer.'

He scoffed. 'Surely you didn't think I'd stay? Why do you want me here, other than to do your wood chopping and some silly notion of redemption?'

'The redemption part is true, Mr Barsom. And my name really is Paige Hanner. Surprised a bit you don't know it.'

'Why would I? I never saw you before last night.'

'That's true, too.'

'Then why do you give a damn about redeeming me? I don't give a damn about redeeming myself.'

She frowned, took a couple steps into the barn. 'I think you do care. In some small way. You can't see it because of your constant state of grief and drunkenness.'

'You don't know me and I doubt you know a damn thing about grief.'

She uttered a humorless chuckle. 'I lied about this place, Mr Barsom. Marshal didn't rent it for me. I did, last spring. I've been in town a spell, keeping an eye on you, as has Betts. And don't think for a damn minute I don't know about grief. I know it 'bout as well as you do.'

'Why bother with me? Why can't you just let me be instead of dragging me out here?'

'Because I owe my sister that much, Mr Barsom. My half-sister, I should say.'

'Who is she?' An odd feeling of

premonition rose in his mind. Something about this woman now seemed slightly . . . familiar.

'She never mentioned my name, Mr Barsom?'

'Who?' The feeling strengthened.

'Tessa.'

'Tessa?' His belly sank. 'No, it ain't possible. She said there was some half-sister back in Colorado.'

'I'm from Colorado, Mr Barsom. As was Tessa. She was my half-sister.'

He shook his head. It couldn't be. And yet this time he got the impression she was telling the truth and genuine pain showed in her eyes.

'She said she had one, but never mentioned a name or talked about her life back there.'

Paige smiled a strained smile, walked to the stall holding the bay and turned away from him. 'You know what the last thing I said to her was, Mr Barsom?' She turned her head to him, eyes bleeding hurt. 'Go to hell. That's what I told her. Right before that I told her I

66

never wanted to see her again and the ironic thing is that's the way it now has to be.'

'She never said anything about it.' His head lowered and he swallowed at the emotion tightening his throat as Tessa's face rose in his mind.

'She wouldn't have, and I can't blame her. We were jealous of each other, the way sisters can be, liking the same men or clothes, competing for them. I was two years older, but in a way I was the one looking up to her and I hated it. We fought — a lot — and the last time it was because she wanted to move away and I couldn't tell her I was angry because I'd miss her. Too much pride for both of us to give in. So we fought before she left. I was furious that she'd even think of leaving, though I knew she was right. She was the brave one. I didn't know she had met you. I found that out later.'

He nodded. 'I was on a case in Colorado. We met at a church supper, but she said she was afraid of her father and he'd never accept me as a manhunter, though I had promised her I would give it up. She said she wanted to leave, go far away.'

A tear slipped down Paige's cheek. 'She and her pa didn't get along, and for a good reason. He . . . drank, and I didn't know what he tried doing to her one night. He confessed it nine months ago, on his death bed. Expected me to forgive him. I couldn't. But I under-stood then why she had wanted to leave so bad. She thought I took up for him, but it wasn't that. I was afraid of him.'

Something in Teel's belly twisted. He hadn't known the reason Tessa hated her father, only that it hurt her too much to talk about and he had respected her wishes. Now it made sense.

'I'm sorry . . . ' was all he could manage to say.

'It's not your fault. Fact, I'm glad you took her away from him. When I learned what happened I left, too, to come here to be with her and tell her I was sorry for being such a coward. I needed her forgiveness. But when I arrived, Marshal Betts told me about you and what had happened.'

'Then you know I'm responsible for her death and redemption ain't possible.'

'We all have our ghosts, Mr Barsom. You want to leave, you're free to go. You're right, I can't keep you here. But I had to try. I can't say I'm sorry to her now, but I owed her something she would have wanted done.'

Paige Hanner turned and walked from the barn, leaving him staring after her. He looked back at the big bay, who nickered, then to the barn entrance again. He knew precious little of Tessa's life before he came into it, and that woman who'd just left was a link to it. He wasn't sure why it mattered, now, but it did. And maybe some firewood was the least he could do to repay the breakfast he'd scattered on the floor.

6

Slade Heath was getting damned tired of his hotel room. While he had the freedom to come and go as he pleased, he knew the lawdog and some of the townsfolk he'd deputized were keeping their eyes on him much more since that day he'd walked out of the marshal's cell. Betts reckoned Slade was responsible somehow for the Barsom place burning down and the death of the manhunter's woman, though he could not prove it and Slade had the perfect alibi, having been standing next to the lawman at the time. But Slade had not avoided a hangman's noose all these years by being stupid, and after the attack on the Barsom place he had decided he and his men would play it even more carefully with their crimes.

But he was growing more antsy by the day and their finances were starting to drain some, despite a number of robberies they'd staged in the area.

He stood by the window in the hotel room, peering out into the noon-day street. Folks moved about on the boardwalks and sunlight glinted from windows and troughs. Peaceful, serene, disgusting. Was like he'd been imprisoned all over again and he didn't care for it a lick.

He glanced back at Jep, who sat at a small table, playing solitaire. Jep seemed entirely at ease with the present lack of activity and never accompanied the others to the saloon for women. Slade had started to suspect for a while the man had gone soft. He had not acted the same since the day they'd attacked the Barsom compound. Slade couldn't abide with any of his men carrying a streak of compassion; there was no place for that in their line of work. That meant Jep might not be trustworthy on bigger jobs, where killing women and children were involved. The man would bear watching.

The other two, Dickson and Harris, were different, entirely ruthless. While Jep sat in a sullen mood, only the cards keeping him company, the other two were likely out with whores they'd engaged for the night. Least that's what Slade figured, based on their usual pattern. If they had pulled some stupid stunt and got their asses tossed in jail, they knew he'd just leave them there and replace them. They also knew if they opened their mouths a bullet would find them before a noose.

Slade had about come to a decision. Coopersville had lost any appeal it ever held for him and he reckoned it was about time they moved on. Of course, before he did so, he had a couple pieces of unfinished business to take care of, and both had to be carried out without witnesses. Slade considered himself a hell of a lot smarter than the average owlhoot. Though suspected of plenty, he didn't have to stay on the run, could set himself up wherever he wanted. No fleeing into Indian territory or hiding out in abandoned shacks for him. He was used to a certain standard of living and intended to keep it that way. The hotel room, while confining in its own right, was comfortable, with gaslights and clean beds, and he reckoned he'd earned that.

So the loose ends, Betts and Barsom, would need to be eliminated carefully.

Of course, he didn't need to take care of either man, as far as them ever pinning any crime on him. But Barsom had witnessed him causing that woman's death and though it was no longer a concern, given the man's reputation for drinking and cowardice, it was a personal score Slade needed to settle. The man had brought him in like a common outlaw and Betts had stuck him in a cell. That could not go unanswered, as far as Slade was concerned. No one did that to him and walked away scot-free. The very thought it had happened ate away at him, had for the last eleven months.

Oh, he had quite enjoyed watching

Barsom suffer the way he had. The once mighty manhunter had become nothing more than a pathetic drunk. For a spell, Slade had reckoned on Barsom coming after him, trying to kill him outright. He had hoped that would be the case, because then he could have put a bullet into him and claimed self-defense and there wouldn't have been a damn thing Betts could have done about it.

But he hadn't. The boy either had a streak of yellow or some kind of moral conscience Slade didn't understand. Whatever the case, Slade had grown tired of watching the boy destroy himself, the way he had grown tired of this cow-stinking town.

'How can you just sit there with them cards all the time?' Slade asked, glancing at Jep, irritation crawling along his hide.

Jep shrugged, laid down another card. 'Better'n gettin' shot at.'

Slade studied the man, who paid him little mind. He got the notion if Jep could figure a way out of the gang, he

74

would be gone. But that wouldn't happen. Only way a man left Slade's gang was by swallowing lead.

The hotel room door opened and Slade's gaze shifted to the two men entering. Dickson had that idiot grin on his face he always had, and Harris was smiling, too, which was unusual.

'Where you been?' Slade asked, not giving a damn.

Dickson doffed his hat, tossed it on a chair by the brass-framed bed.

'We been following Barsom,' Dickson said and Slade's eyes narrowed on him.

'Followin' him where? He ain't missed a night in the saloon in eleven months and always goes back to the same place. Fact, I figure it's about time he disappears from there and the only one who might miss him will be joinin' him.'

Jep looked up from his cards and Dickson and Harris exchanged glances.

'What do you mean?' Jep asked, coming to his feet.

'Figure I'm tired of this town. We're

going to kill Barsom and Betts and move on.'

''Cept you'll have to kill some woman, too,' Dickson said, a note of expectation in his tone.

'What the hell are you talkin' about, Dickson?' Slade asked. 'Why were you followin' Barsom?'

Dickson licked his lips. 'He was in the saloon last night. We decided to keep him company.'

'I told you to keep away from him for the time being.' Slade's face darkened with anger. He swore he was a hair's breadth away from moving on without any of these sorry sonsofbitches and finding a whole new gang.

'We was just havin' some fun with the sonofabitch, Slade.' A glint of worry sparked in Dickson's dull eyes.

'See to it you do what I tell you. You know better than to be makin' decisions on your own.'

Harris' face had sobered and he paled. Dickson nodded, swallowing.

'I reckon you'll be glad we did.'

'Get to it, Dickson. My patience is about plumb wore as thin as it gets.'

'Marshal came in, had a woman with him,' Dickson said, hastily.

'So?' Slade's gaze held the man, made him shift feet.

'They took Barsom out of the bar and put him in the back of a buckboard. Harris and I waited in an alley across the street after the marshal sent us out of the place. The woman took him.'

'Took him?' Maybe the stupid son-ofabitch had done something right in following them after all.

'Out to the old Longworth cabin. I reckon she lives there, now. Marshal helped her get him into the place, then left. Barsom's still there. Saw him chopping wood.'

What the hell? Slade thought. Barsom was a drunk; chopping wood for some woman didn't seem right.

'Who is she?' Slade asked.

Dickson shrugged. 'Don't know. Ain't seen her before but seems like she's been in the place a spell and Betts was right friendly with her. Think she's sobering up Barsom for some reason.'

Why would she? Slade ran a hand over his stubbly chin, brow knitting. He didn't like it one damn bit. Barsom as a pathetic drunk was not a problem; Barsom sober might be. He had a reputation before losing his wife, after all, and Slade figured he'd probably deserved it.

'Reckon you did right, after all,' Slade said and the grin came back to Dickson's face.

'He's still out there.'

Slade went back to the window, peered out, remained silent for long moments. 'I reckon we need to find out who this woman is before we kill Barsom. I don't want complications.'

'How you gonna do that?' Harris asked.

Slade's face went grim. 'We're going to ride right on out there and introduce ourselves. It's the neighborly thing to do.'

'What if Barsom decides to take a

shot at us?' Dickson said.

'He won't. He was gonna do that he would have by now.' Fact was, though he said that, Slade wasn't entirely sure Barsom might not grow a set and do just that — and that was why he needed to know exactly who this woman was and what she wanted with the man-hunter before he made a move.

Turning from the window, Slade noticed the sullen look deepening on Jep's face. The man hadn't said a word but disapproval showed in his eyes.

'You got somethin' to say, Jep?' Slade asked.

'Why don't we just ride out and leave Barsom alone, Slade?' Jep said. 'We done enough to him and he ain't never going to be the same. He can't accuse us of nothin', now.'

'You goin' soft, Jep?' Slade asked. 'You know I don't cotton to Nancy boys.'

Jep shifted his feet, shook his head slowly. 'Just don't think it's worth the risk.'

Slade smiled, an instant before his fist came up and took Jep full across the jaw. The outlaw flew backward over a chair, hit the floor hard.

Slade nodded to the two other men, then to Jep. Harris and Dickson, grinning like fools, grabbed Jep's arms and hoisted him to his feet.

Slade buried a fist in Jep's belly, doubling the outlaw over, then hit him with an uppercut.

Harris and Dickson dropped him, and Jep hit the floor, curled up, blood snaking from his lip.

Slade knelt before him, forearm across a knee. 'You tell me if you're goin' soft, Jep, and I'll leave you right here, let you go your own way.' That would never happen. He would put a bullet in Jep the minute the man responded with a yes.

'No.' A cough wracked Jep's body. He spat a stream of saliva and blood. 'I ain't goin' soft.'

'You certain of that, Jep? I can't abide by soft.'

'No . . . ' Jep mumbled. 'Never.'

Slade stood, looked to his other two men, who were watching with amusement.

'Saddle up,' Slade said. 'We're joinin' the welcoming committee.'

7

It had been a long time since Teel Barsom had done the type of physical labor it took to run a ranch, and given the amount of whiskey he'd consumed in the last eleven months it came as no surprise to him his arms were trembling by the time he finished chopping wood. He brought the ax down a final time, burying the head in the stump. Despite the coolness of the day, sweat ran down his face and sides. Using his forearm, he mopped perspiration from his brow, then picked up the two sides of the log he'd just split. The rest, he had stacked at the side of the house. He went to the stack, cradled a couple more pieces in his arms, then headed for the house.

Had anyone asked, he couldn't have said why he had bothered doing the woman's bidding. He supposed he owed her for the night's lodgings — though he had certainly not asked her to abduct him — and the tray of biscuits and pot of coffee he'd scattered on the floor. But it went beyond that. While it was different from his own, he understood the guilt she felt over losing her sister. His own, he had brought on himself, but hers was a misunderstanding between family members, something, had Tessa still been alive, that could have been easily patched. But Paige was too late and she would blame herself when it was not her fault. So maybe in some odd way he felt obligated to her.

She reminded him of Tessa in small ways. He reckoned some of that came with the knowledge Paige was Tessa's half-sister, but it went deeper, now that he had sobered up and thought about it. The hair color was close, the way she smiled, the glint in her eyes, and the attitude. Tessa had never been one to put up with his cowflop and it was plain this woman was cut from the same cloth. Maybe even more so. The physical resemblance beyond that was fleeting.

He climbed the steps to the porch, noticing he was shaking even more and the nearly overwhelming desire for a drink took him. His head still banged, but now with only a muffled drumbeat, and his belly wavered between nausea and hunger. He wondered where she kept the key to the padlocked door in the barn.

He reached the door, managed to open it without dropping any of the wood, and kicked it shut behind him. He set the wood next to the fireplace, gaze momentarily touching on the Winchester mounted on pegs above the mantel.

A shudder shook his lanky frame as a chill washed through him. He folded his arms about himself, wondering how the hell he could be hot and cold at the same time. Nausea rushed back, and though he managed to keep his stomach down, it was a struggle. He went to the couch, sat, leaning forward, body wracked with chills, sweat dripping from his brow. He didn't know quite how long he stayed that way, but when he looked up, Paige stood next to him, draping a blanket over his shoulders. He had not heard her approach. She gave him a small smile and he gripped the edges of the blanket, pulling it to his chin.

'Jesus,' he said. 'I don't know what's wrong with me. Never used to get this way chopping wood.'

She gave him a small laugh. 'Never used to drink your meals, either, I bet. You're dryin' out, Mr Barsom. Takes a spell and you'll go through hell for a while.'

'I don't want to dry out,' he said, steadying his voice. If he dried out, he'd have to face the pain, the ghosts, the decisions that had lost him all he gave a damn about.

'What's your choice, then?' she asked, folding her arms beneath her breasts. With the afternoon sunlight streaming through the windows, back-lighting her hair, she looked somehow angelic, lovely, and he chastised himself for even thinking such a thing. He'd had no thoughts of other women since Tessa's death and had never been with one of the bar girls, no matter how much the loneliness had consumed him.

'There doesn't need to be a choice,' he said.

'Perhaps there doesn't, but there is one. Yours is to stop pitying yourself and face what happened, the way I've had to, or drink yourself to death. Or maybe you won't even have to wait that long, because sooner or later those men who attacked you last night are going to get tired of the cat and mouse. You don't really think men like that will let you live, do you?'

'You know.' His voice came out a whisper.

She nodded. 'I know who they are and I know the marshal suspects they had something to do with Tessa's death and your ranch burning down.'

His eyes rose to meet hers and he searched for the hate in her soul that should have been reflected on her face. 'Then you know I'm to blame.'

'Are you?' she asked, tone serious.

'Yes.' His voice came so low he wasn't certain whether he had spoken.

'You are responsible for the actions of men who rob and kill? Men who make their living by taking from innocent folks?'

'You don't understand. I wouldn't have taken that man in — '

'He would have killed someone else and kept killing. That was not a wrong choice, Mr Barsom.'

'Other choices were.' The chills stopped and deep within the pain of loss rose up again, as it inevitably did when he went too long between drinks.

'And your answer to that is to hide in the bottle?' Her tone hardened and her blue eyes bore into him. In that instant her resemblance to Tessa was stronger or perhaps for some reason he couldn't grasp he wanted to see it there.

'I'm not hiding.'

'Aren't you? You're killing yourself,

that's for certain. Do you think Tessa would want that? She saw something special in you, Mr Barsom. She must have to run to you, to make a new life here. You lookin' to prove her wrong? Make a mockery of her memory?'

'Shut the hell up!' he yelled, and sprang from the couch, throwing off the blanket. What goddamn right did this woman have bringing him here and speaking to him that way? What right did she have to use his loss against him?

No, that wasn't fair. She wasn't using it against him, she was just stating the truth. He was just angry because perhaps . . . perhaps she was seeing something in him he no longer wanted to be there. A will to survive.

'Truth stings, don't it, Mr Barsom? I know . . . *knew*, my sister. I didn't listen to her and look where it got me? Alone. With no chance of ever telling her how sorry I was for being such a fool. You need to listen to her, do what she would want you to do.'

'She's gone, don't you understand

that? She's gone because of a stupid mistake I made and I can't listen to her anymore.'

'You can, Mr Barsom. Her words, her memory, are part of you, like they're part of me. You know she wouldn't want this for you. You know she wouldn't want you to live your life blaming yourself and drinking yourself into an early grave.'

He shook his head, confusion gripping him. Dammit, he needed a drink.

A sound interrupted before he could say anything to the young woman who stared at him, awaiting a response. Hoofbeats, muffled but growing closer. Three, maybe four riders.

'You expecting company?' he said, and by the surprised look on her face he could see the answer. He moved to the window, peered out, Paige coming up beside him. She smelled of rosewater and biscuits and he wondered why he even noticed such a thing.

'Oh, hell . . . ' he whispered, gaze locking on four men in dusters who appeared at the edge of the property. They rode straight for the cabin and though he could not see their faces, he knew from the set of their frames in the saddle who they were. 'They must have followed you here last night, seen you bring me in.'

She shook her head. 'I saw no one, but it doesn't matter if they know.'

He peered at her with rising anger. 'The hell it don't! I'm responsible for enough death. Now that sonofabitch has his sights on you.'

'You're jumpin' to conclusions, Mr Barsom.'

'Why else would they be here? They're lookin' to see what you want with me.'

'Then I will face them, tell them you left.' She moved towards the door.

'What the hell do you think you're doin'? Those men killed your sister. They won't think twice about adding you to the list.'

She turned to him, gave him a look that said she was not afraid of those men in the least. 'The marshal told me this man, Heath, goes to great lengths to leave no clues to his crimes. He is riding in here in broad daylight and the marshal knows both of us are here. That man knows he knows. He did not come here to kill me or you, at least not yet. He came for information.'

She was likely right, but it was only a temporary reprieve and now that Heath knew this woman had helped him she was in danger. He wasn't going to let what had happened to Tessa happen to her.

He went to the fireplace, lifted the rifle from the pegs, then turned back to her. 'This loaded?'

She nodded, one hand on the doorhandle. 'Stay in here.'

'The hell I will!' He started towards her.

'You are not in any condition to face this man yet. He would shoot you where you stand if he thought you were a threat and it would be self-defense. You'd be giving him what he wants.'

'I can't just let you go out there alone.'

'Watch from the window. You got any shootin' skills left it won't be much of a shot if he tries something.'

She opened the door as he went to the window. She was right, but some not-so-small part of him hoped Heath would give him a reason to blow him out of the saddle.

8

Paige Hanner didn't like the fact that Slade Heath and his men were riding up to her cabin one bit. She had expected they would come, but not so soon, and neither she nor Teel Barsom were ready for a confrontation yet. She needed time to sober him up, make him understand life was worth going on with, give him a cause to fight for — the same cause she'd clung to to preserve her own sanity when she'd learned what had happened to her sister. That these men were here meant she had misjudged Heath and the imbeciles who rode with him. One of them must have taken a notion to follow her last night.

She paused on the edge of the porch, blue eyes locking on the four riders closing the distance. Hate surged in her heart. She wanted those sonsofbitches dead, though she knew it would not bring her sister back or alleviate the loss and guilt she felt over Tessa's murder.

She wanted them dead but she would settle for justice.

She came down the steps, legs shaking, though she concealed her fear. She refused to let those men intimidate her, see her scared. She refused to let any man do so ever again. She had never told Tessa how much their pa frightened her. That had been part of the problem the day Tessa left, though she had not told Barsom that. Her fear of the old man had caused her to stick her head in the sand, ignore things that were right in front of her eyes. She'd been afraid of him and afraid of running away from him. She always had the strange notion he would find her wherever she went, drag her back like some sinful child. Tessa was braver than she in that way. She wished she could go back and change that, but she couldn't, and her plans here were the only way she saw to make amends and beg her sister's forgiveness.

Those plans included Teel Barsom.

He was different than she'd thought he would be. She had watched him quite a spell, but from a distance, and seen a pitiable drunk, and a mission she needed to complete. She hadn't expected to see such pain and regret in his eyes. There was far more to him than she anticipated, and she perceived something still vital and silver in the man she knew he did not see within himself.

It would make sacrificing him, as she had known was a possibility from the start, much more difficult. That's part of the reason she'd made him stay in the house. A hesitation on her part.

It worried her, perhaps even frightened her. It threatened to change things and her plan had been black and white. She was beginning to see what Tessa saw in him.

She pushed that out of her mind for the moment, and forced herself to take steady confident steps down the dirt pathway towards the approaching riders, though inside she felt anything but confident.

She had the derringer in her skirt pocket, but these four were killers, all heeled. Hate swept through her again, steeling her composure. Killers. Murderers. And they would pay. But not today. Of course, if they decided to kill or violate her, any plan she'd made would go to hell. She glanced backward to the front window. She hoped Barsom could pull that trigger and still hit what he aimed at if it came down to it.

Heath would not be blatantly riding in here if he intended to kill them, she assured herself, as she had Barsom a few minutes earlier. He wanted information, but he was going to leave empty-handed.

The riders drew closer, the thunder of their mounts' hoofs beating the browning grass flat, kicking up clumps as they slowed. She walked right out into the yard before them, face tight, unflinching, blue eyes concealing the hate she had for them. No use tipping them off. As far as they knew, she could be some church do-gooder. The thought struck her as funny. She'd never set foot inside a church and, considering her plan here, she was about as far from being a do-gooder as the Devil himself. At least, that's the way she viewed it.

The riders drew up, Slade Heath in the lead. She stood her ground as his mount came to a halt only a few feet before her. His gaze raked her full figure, not without a glint of lust. Those eyes. Dead. Vacant. Merciless. She had never seen eyes like his and they were in stark contrast to the man inside her cabin. As if the outlaw had read her mind, his gaze lifted to one of the front windows, riveted there. Did he suspect Teel was poised at the sill with her rifle or had he glimpsed movement or sunlight glinting off metal?

'What do you want here?' she asked, trying to sway his attention from the house. Even if a confrontation started, Teel might get Slade if he could still aim worth a damn, maybe one other. She might take out a second or third with the derringer, but her death would be certain. She didn't care. As long as Slade died, it would be worth it, and she couldn't rightly ask anything of Teel that didn't apply to herself.

Slade's gaze shifted to her and a peculiar grin came to his lips, the scar, running from one corner of his mouth to his ear wriggling like a living thing.

'My men told me we had a new neighbor, so we came to welcome you.' Beside Slade, the man named Dickson chuckled like an idiot child.

'Welcoming committees don't usually come so well heeled, Mr Heath.' She locked gazes with the outlaw, refusing to flinch.

'You know who I am?'

She nodded. 'Don't everybody in Coopersville?'

He canted his head a notch. 'I reckon that's a truism. Puts me at a disadvantage, then, ma'am. And I'm not partial to such a position.'

'I don't reckon you are, Mr Heath.' She studied him, trying to gage him. He had shown more smarts than most outlaws, but she was certain she saw chinks — in patience, restrained reaction, cockiness. She might be able to use one or all of those against him when the time came . . . *if* it came.

'Who are you, ma'am?' Slade asked, a hint of exasperation in his tone. He wasn't used to parity; he was used to cat and mouse, with him as the cat.

'My name's Paige Hanner. You've done welcomed me so now you can just ride on back to where you came from.'

His face tightened a fraction. 'That's your name, ma'am. Why are you here?'

It wasn't what he wanted to ask, she felt certain. He wanted to know what business she intended with that man in her home.

'I live here, Mr Heath. Coopersville seemed like a peaceful place to settle down, at least until the likes of you rode in.'

Slade flinched. It was only for a blink, but she caught it. He was struggling with being cordial.

'You live here alone, ma'am?' His

voice came a hair lower, darker.

'I do, as if it is any of your concern.'

She could see in his eyes he clearly did not believe her. 'Well, no, ma'am, my man Dickson here tells me that might not be the case.'

She laughed, and was pleased with the flicker of annoyance that crossed his face. 'Like I said, as if it's any of your concern.'

Slade shifted in the saddle, stared unwaveringly, trying to make her back down. She didn't budge and her new-found courage gave her a surge of satisfaction. If only she'd stood up to her pa this way, she might have been with Tessa, able to protect her from these men.

'Well, I'm afraid it just might be my business.' His voice now lost all of its pleasant inflection. 'Dickson says you might be harboring a dangerous man out here. I'm checking strictly for your own welfare.'

Her gaze went to Dickson, then back to Slade. 'Saw your man at the saloon last night, Mr Heath. I take it he enjoys taunting defenseless drunks.'

'Nothing defenseless about Teel Barsom, ma'am, or didn't you know he's a professional killer? Rumor has it he even killed his own wife and burned down his ranch to hide the fact. Dangerous and loco, I'd say. Just don't want *you* endin' up in the same condition.'

Slade emphasized the last, making the threat clear. At the mention of Tessa's murder, blaming it on Teel, she wanted to kill Slade right where he sat, but she held her temper.

'Thank you kindly for your concern, Mr Heath.' She put no sincerity in her tone. 'But I can take care of myself, so please leave.'

'He in there, ma'am?' Slade wasn't about to back down, but neither was she.

'No.'

He sighed an exasperated sigh. Good. He knew she was lying, but the question was, what would he do about it?

'Maybe he threatened you and you're

just afraid to say anything. I best take a look inside and see for myself.' He started to climb from his horse, but her hand darted into her skirt and came out with the derringer, brought it to aim on his chest, stopping him.

Two of his men, the two from the bar, started to go for their guns. The third sat strangely still, appearing almost uninterested.

Slade shook his head, held up a hand to stop them from drawing. She knew it, then: Slade had spotted Teel at the window with a rifle and this wasn't the time of his choosing to force a fight. He liked overwhelming odds, sneak attacks.

'What do you want with that man, Miss Hanner?' Slade's voice now came hard, all pretense gone.

'That falls into the realm of none of your business, Mr Heath.' She kept the derringer aimed at his chest, didn't shake. It occurred to her such a small gun was a hell of a thing to rely on when it came to life or death.

'Teel Barsom ain't long for this

world, Miss Hanner. Would be a pity if you joined him.'

Something in his manner told her that decision had already been made. He would kill her when he found the odds to his advantage.

He reined around, signaling his men to do the same, and heeled his horse into a gallop.

She watched them go, a case of the shudders letting loose now they were riding away.

But it was only a temporary reprieve. They would be back and next time she wouldn't be as lucky. Things had to be stepped up. She lowered the derringer, slipped it back into her pocket, and went back towards the house, hoping the wager she'd placed on that man inside wasn't a fool's bet.

★   ★   ★

From the window, Teel Barsom watched the young woman walk down the steps and towards the approaching riders, his admiration for her growing with each step. She was one woman, alone, facing outlaws, and she looked like she was walking into a church supper.

He eased the window open a couple of inches, rested the Winchester's barrel on the sill. Sweat dampened his palms and his hands carried a slight tremble. He wanted to leave, find a bottle, but this was his fault in a way, despite the fact that she had brought him here of her own free will. Those men wanted to know why he was here and maybe if he hadn't been such a useless drunk she wouldn't have put herself in a position to risk her life.

Why *was* she risking it? Just what did she want from him? No one bothered trying to save another unless there was something in it for them. Except Tessa. He recollected her kindness, her need to help others, even small critters she fed at the ranch. But this woman was not Tessa, despite superficial resemblances. She had to want something. And he wagered it had something to do with those men.

His gaze narrowed as the riders drew up before her. For a moment, Slade's eyes rose to the window and Teel felt as if the man was somehow peering right through him. Did the outlaw see him? The rifle? Teel felt certain he did.

Teel's hands tightened on the Winchester. It would be so very easy just to pull the trigger, blast Slade out of the saddle. Though he wasn't a killer, he could, in his sober state, imagine himself just barely touching the trigger, easing it in. He could smell the acrid gunsmoke and hear the crash of thunder in his mind.

He wanted to kill him. Lordamighty, he did. Avenge Tessa. But he knew she would not want that and any random shot, regardless of whether it killed Slade, would risk ending the life of the young woman out there.

Judas Priest. Things were so much easier when he was drunk.

The young woman's arm suddenly came up, a derringer in her hand, aimed at the outlaw, pulling Teel from his thoughts. His heart skipped a beat and his hands shook harder. Sweat trickled from his brow.

He centered the Winchester's aim on the outlaw's chest. He had no delusions about his skills after a year of drink and would go for the largest body area if gunfire broke out. He would indeed kill the man if it came down to protecting that young woman's life, though likely he would not be able to save her. A selfish fleeting thought made him almost wish Slade would try something.

Muscles balled on either side of his jaw and the minutes dragged by. His palms went from moist to slick with sweat. Slade was not going to press a fight, that became evident, and he was relieved, despite his passing thought.

At last, the riders turned, headed away. The woman stood stock still, watching them go, and Teel's heart slowed. He pulled the rifle out of the window, stood, his entire body shaking.

Paige opened the door and entered,

shutting it behind her. She glanced at him.

'They know you're here. He wants to know why.'

'You tell him?' Teel went to the fireplace, placed the Winchester back on the pegs.

'Nothing I do is any of that man's business.'

He turned back to her. 'He'll be back. You know that, don't you? And next time he won't back off so easy.'

She chuckled, not much humor in it. 'That was easy?'

'Compared to what he is capable of, it was.' Teel's voice came dark, the memory of his burned-out ranch rising in his mind.

'I'll ride into town to see the marshal, tell him what happened.'

'Won't help.' Teel went back to the couch, fell on to it, legs weak.

'Maybe not. But that man don't like witnesses or links to his crimes. So can't hurt to let it be known he came a-callin'.'

Teel looked up at her. 'You don't know that man, what kind of a monster you're dealin' with.'

'I know what I saw out there. He don't leave witnesses, but he's no different from others of his kind in some ways. The fact that you're here and I'm helpin' you will stick in his craw. He'll make a move sooner than he rightly expected to. He'll get cocky because of what he did to you last time, and running free so long has made him think he's untouchable. He's not.'

'All of which tells me you want more out of me than redemption.'

She smiled. 'Maybe I'm just a do-gooder, Mr Barsom. Tessa and I both liked helpin' folks. Made us feel better about not being able to help ourselves.'

'You seem plenty able to help yourself, now.'

'I've changed a lot in the last year. Losing what's important to you will do that.'

'Maybe you should just tell me the truth.'

She went to the window, gazed out. 'There's a fence that needs mending on the north side, Mr Barsom. If you could see your way to it while I ride in to see the marshal, I'd be obliged.'

'There's a spare horse in your barn; I could leave.'

She turned to him, smiled. 'You could. Horse was meant for your disposal, since you sold yours eleven months ago.' With that, she went to the door, stepped outside and shut it behind her, leaving him wondering just why the hell he didn't want to leave.

9

'How is he?' Marshal Betts asked after Paige stepped into his office.

She closed the door, then slid her hat from her raspberry curls, to let it hang at her back. 'He's comin' along faster than I thought he would. I think deep down he wants a direction, he just don't know it yet.'

'He suspect anything?' The marshal, sitting behind his desk, shifted in his chair, then took a sip from the tin cup holding coffee on his desk.

'He knows I got a hidden reason for wanting him there, but he don't know what it is. He's curious, and I didn't think he would be.'

'Maybe he's not as far gone as I thought.'

She glanced at the lawman, then went to the window and peered out at the sun-dappled main street. A few passers-by strolled along the boardwalks, but she saw no sign of Slade Heath or his men. She had half-expected Slade to leave one behind, follow anyone who came out of the cabin, but she'd spotted no one dogging her on the ride into town. She was just as glad, too; she'd had enough of those bastards for one day.

'He's a man who lost the one thing that meant the most to him, Betts. I reckon I can understand that all too well. He took to the bottle, I took to revenge.'

'He might not be so eager to stay around if he knew what you had in mind for him, and that he might not live through it.'

She paused, wondering if maybe her plan wasn't so all-fired important, now. She hadn't expected to see Teel Barsom as a man. She had expected to blame him for his part in her sister's death and maybe she had been wrong about that, her judgment clouded by grief and fury at the men who were responsible. The pain and loss in his eyes ... they weren't the marks of a man responsible for anything other than caring.

'I'm thinkin' this idea maybe ain't so necessary as I thought it was.' She glanced back at the marshal, whose brows arched.

'You sayin' you don't want Heath punished for what he did?'

'No ... no, I'm not sayin' that. When I rode in here last spring and you told me what happened to Tessa, that's all I could think about, Slade Heath breathin' his last. I planned for it, watched my sister's husband, watched Slade and his men. I still want him dead, but maybe setting Barsom up to do it after the condition he's been in for so long isn't the answer I thought it was.'

'If it weren't for that boy, Slade would be still in a cell.'

'And his men would still be free and my sister would still be dead. It wouldn't change anything.'

'It would mean the man responsible would be payin' for his crime.'

She uttered a lifeless laugh. 'It would mean he was payin' for a crime, not Tessa's murder. He was in your cell when it happened, I recollect right.'

'He ordered it, he had to have. His men carried out his orders.'

'But they would not be in jail. They'd be free to continue robbin' and killin', maybe even break Slade out.'

The marshal ran a hand over his chin. 'But they ain't smart like Slade. They would have got caught or killed. 'Sides, at least havin' Slade would be somethin'. That boy just let him go.'

She watched a wagon rattle down the rutted street, two folks, a man and a woman, holding hands in the driver's seat, laughing. 'You ever asked yourself why he did it, Marshal?' She looked over a shoulder at him. 'Why he just up and changed his mind after bringing Heath in?'

The lawman shrugged. 'Don't have to. Answer's obvious, ain't it? He turned coward. Bettin' Slade's men threatened him.'

'What do you think they threatened him with? A manhunter who'd spent years tracking down wanted men isn't the type to just cower under a threat.'

Another shrug. 'The obvious — the ranch, his family.'

She nodded. 'That man in my parlor right now ain't a coward, Betts. I can tell you that much. I know cowards. I was one. He's in pain. He misses his wife and blames himself. I had to bet, I'd wager Slade's men threatened Tessa and Barsom compromised himself to save her. They killed her just the same to let him know he wasn't ever to make the mistake of bringing Heath in again. Teel Barsom did what he did because he loved his wife and put her before his own conscience and reputation. I can't fault him for that.'

'Sounds to me like you're goin' soft on him.' The marshal frowned, took another sip from his cup.

The words took her aback, and she averted her eyes from the lawdog, peered back out into the street. 'What would his death serve?' she asked after a dragging moment.

'If it took Slade Heath off this world, then maybe justice.'

'I thought that a few months ago, hell, even a few days ago. But are two innocent lives, his and Tessa's, worth the outlaw's one?'

'Slade's responsible for other deaths, other crimes. I can't prove them, but there's no doubt.'

'Ain't arguin' that point, Betts. He needs to pay for what he done. But there must be another way. I . . . I don't feel right giving Barsom his life back only to risk it, now that I've met him.'

'Jesus, Paige, you're talkin' like a woman getting too attached to a man she barely knows, a man who as far as I'm concerned, committed an act of cowardice.'

She turned her head back to him, irritation riding her nerves, studied him a moment. 'You know in your heart that sooner or later Slade's going to come after you because you put him in jail.

You sure you don't want this to go through because you're afraid of that happening?'

The marshal's face flushed crimson and she knew she had hit a sore spot. He did fear Slade coming after him and would have been much more comfortable with the outlaw and his men dead or in cells.

'I resent that, Miss Hanner.'

'But it don't change the facts none, does it? And it don't make either you or Barsom less of a man for being afraid of the likes of Slade Heath. Only a fool wouldn't be. I am.'

The marshal appeared to deflate in his chair. 'Maybe you're right. Just damn goads me to see Slade walkin' the streets and Barsom drinkin' his life away.'

She nodded, wrapped her arms about herself. 'Slade came out to the ranch today. He knows Barsom is there and wants to know why. One of his men must have followed us last night.'

The marshal's face bleached. 'Oh, Christ on a crutch.' He rubbed his

116

chin, eyes darting. 'That might mean you won't have time to get Barsom ready, anyway. Slade even thinks for a minute Barsom's going to return to what he used to be, he'll kill him . . . and me.' He peered harder at her. 'And you.'

She nodded. 'Aware of it. Barsom will get himself ready. Don't ask me how I know it, but I do. He's not ready to die yet. He's just needin' a reason to go on without Tessa.'

'Give him one, then. Other than Slade.'

Her eyes narrowed. 'What's that s'posed to mean?'

He chuckled, a hint of nervousness in it. 'I reckon you didn't tell Slade that Barsom was there and what you wanted him for.'

She shook her head. 'He backed down this time. He wasn't ready for an open fight, didn't expect any resistance from a woman. I won. This time. Don't think he'll wait long, though, to put the odds in his favor.'

'Keep your eyes open. I don't want to see what happened to your sister happen to you. You best think about setting Barsom on them the way you planned, whether you got feelings for him or not.'

A prickle of annoyance went through her nerves. She suddenly wasn't sure what to do. It had been so clear to her when she'd ridden in, but now . . . now she wondered if she hadn't bitten off more than she could chew.

★ ★ ★

'Don't understand why you let that woman get the upper hand on us, Slade,' Dickson said sitting at the table near the window in the hotel room. He tossed down a losing hand as Harris, fingers interlocked, swept the small pile of coins and bills towards him, a grin on his face.

Slade Heath, sitting in a chair, a rolled cigarette between his lips, glared at his man, thinking about putting a bullet in him. If Dickson weren't so stupid and didn't follow orders — mostly — he might have.

Because he was goddamned annoyed with himself for having backed down to a lowly woman. But to kill her and Barsom right then and there, assuming he and his men survived, then returning to town to kill the marshal, were not odds and operations to his liking. That didn't mean it didn't stick in his craw. He would get even with her before he buried her, that was for damn sure.

Slade plucked the cigarette from his lips. 'You're damn lucky you put me on to Barsom being out there, Dickson, or you'd be dead where you're sittin'.'

Dickson and Harris's expressions sobered. Jep sat at the other side of the table, playing solitaire, appearing uninterested in the proceedings.

'Didn't mean nothin' by it, Slade.' Dickson's voice held a note of fear and Slade liked that.

'Barsom was in the window with a rifle. I saw the sun flash off the barrel. We'da tried anything he would have got one or more of us and the girl would have got another.'

'Who the hell is she?' Harris asked, shuffling the cards.

'That's a right good question.' Slade took a draw from his cigarette, blew the smoke out. 'Got no notion. But it won't matter where she's goin'.'

'What you reckon she wants with Barsom? He's just a drunk.' Dickson shook his head, swept up the cards Harris had dealt him.

'He is now . . . but he wasn't always. He returns to what he used to be we got nothing to take away from him this time. A man driven by revenge is a problem.'

'Wouldn't he have already done that if he was goin' to?' Dickson asked.

Slade shook his head. 'He was too focused on his grief, then got caught in the bottle. Might be different if he sobers up now.'

'What about the girl? We could threaten her.' Dickson plucked at his cards, rearranging their order in his hand.

Slade wondered, but quickly dismissed the thought. 'This girl, he just met her. Not like his wife. His type will care about the life of someone innocent, but the question is, how much? Too soon to count on that.'

'Then maybe he'll just go back to the bottle.'

Slade drew in another drag on his cigarette, let the smoke trickle out. 'You ever seen a man who's truly lost everything, Dickson?'

Dickson shook his head. 'Reckon not.'

'They ain't like you or me. They go loco. You can't scare 'em. That gives them an advantage. I can't have that.'

'What do we do about it?' Harris asked, looking up from his cards.

'We move against him and the girl. And that no-account marshal, too. But we do it on my terms, not theirs. We don't wait till they come after us. I got myself a notion that girl is after me for something I did to someone she cares about. She's got no other reason to help Barsom and put herself in my sights.'

'But they got no proof of anything,' Dickson said. 'We didn't leave nothin' at that ranch by the time we got done with it.'

Slade laughed. 'A man driven by revenge don't need proof. He'll dog us until he finds some. We're going to clean up loose ends and leave Coopersville, and get rid of Barsom before he figures out revenge is exactly what he wants.'

10

Teel Barsom reined the pinto to a halt a few hundred yards from the burned-out remains of his ranch, belly knotting and a wave of grief washing over him. Instead of leaving, simply riding away from Paige Hanner's cabin and returning to his life in a stupor at the saloon, he had come here. And he wasn't entirely sure why, other than he knew Slade Heath would come for him, and when that time came it would be better if he had retrieved the one piece of his manhunting past he kept on these grounds.

The place hadn't changed over the past eleven months. He'd refused to let anyone touch it, leaving it as a pile of blackened beams and the scorched remnants of a life taken and another never to be lived; a melancholy shrine, and a reflection of what he now was inside.

Late afternoon sun, just beginning its dip towards the low western hills, fell over the ruins and browning grass in weird serrated patches, and a cool breeze seemed pregnant with the whispers of lost promises.

He dismounted, legs trembling, but stronger than they had been earlier in the day, and made his way forward to a parcel of grass upon which he had erected a teepee-like structure. He'd built it out of pieces he'd gathered from the ruins, something he'd learned in his manhunter days in encounters with friendly Indians. In front of the structure was a circle of rocks, ash piled within. The camp-fire he built every night when he staggered back here from the saloon, or at least on the nights he didn't pass out along the way.

Paige had asked him where he spent his nights. He spent them here, close to Tessa, as close as was still possible.

He went to a small headstone he'd had the funeral man in town make for him and peered down at the name carved into it: Tessa Barsom. He'd buried her on the land she'd loved, so he could keep her close, and many a folk had accused him of losing his mind for doing so. He didn't care. Sometimes, in the dead of the night, in moments of consciousness, he swore he heard her voice on the wind.

'You *are* a pathetic drunk,' he said, voice damning. 'Townsfolk are right. Is that what you think she'd want?'

He fell to his knees, a great wave of sorrow surging through him. His fingers reached out, touched her name on the stone. Her face flashed through his mind, then came an image of her standing at the counter in their ranch kitchen, making biscuits. A smudge of flour dotted her nose and a smile was on his face as he came in from tending the few head of longhorns that had now wandered off, or been sold to other ranches. He reached out to brush the flour from her face, but the image dissolved and all he touched was cold stone.

'I did what I thought was right to protect you,' he said, drawing back his hand. 'I knew it was wrong but I thought it was worth your life, Tessa. I'd do it again, I swear I would, if I thought it would save you.'

But it would not. It hadn't then and as many times as he relived it in his mind it never would. Slade Heath was not a man who kept promises; he was a man driven by greed and vindictiveness. And Teel should have known better. He should have been home protecting her instead of at the jail letting that murderer walk free.

'Why?' Teel said, voice rising, heart pounding. His hand balled into a fist and he rose to his feet. He looked up at the sky through bleary eyes.

'Why did you have to kill her?' he screamed. His fist came up, knuckles white from the strain of clenching, and he shook it at the sky. 'She never did a damn thing to you! I did! Why did you have to kill her, you sonofabitch? I let you go. I gave you what you wanted.

You still took her from me!'

A tear streaked down his face. He fell back to his knees before the gravestone, then slumped forward. Pounding a fist against the ground, he struggled to force the overwhelming fury and grief away, but it screamed through every fiber, every nerve.

'Why did you have to kill her?' he muttered over and over, sobs wracking his body.

Would there ever come a day when he could recollect her with the simple joy he'd once felt? Without the awful sense of loss and feeling he'd been cheated out of a lifetime?

Not with Slade free. Tessa would never rest in peace until Slade paid for his crimes, and Teel had been so mired in his own pity and self-loathing he had done nothing to give her that peace.

Another mistake in a line of them.

Time dragged. At last his head came up and he breathed a shuddering breath.

'Slade!' he yelled and the name

seemed to echo across the land like the laughter of demons.

Silence came back, mocking. He peered at the gravestone, lost in time and space, unmoving for nearly a half hour.

'I miss you, Tessa. Lord, I do,' he whispered at last, coming to his feet, a leaden sense of emptiness permeating the surroundings and his lanky frame.

He turned away from the marker, unable to look at it another moment. Damnit, he needed a drink. Things were so much easier when whiskey blunted his pain, his memories. He should have gone to the saloon instead of coming here.

But a drink wouldn't change the other problem he now had, would it? Slade was not going to let go of what had happened earlier today with Tessa's sister, nor was he going to chance letting Teel get back to a level where he posed a threat. It was only a matter of time until the outlaw moved on him and Paige Hanner.

Teel had known all along sooner or

later a man like Slade would tire of this town and when he did he would not leave loose ends. The arrest had been an affront, one not considered excused until Teel was dead.

He had known it and not cared, because his own life meant nothing without Tessa. That's what he'd told himself. And he'd meant it. He'd been ready to die. But Tessa's sister . . .

She's not your problem . . .

She had taken him against his will, forced him to sober up. She'd brought Slade down on herself. Whatever she wanted out of him, he couldn't give it to her. He owed her nothing, and that was that.

She's Tessa's blood . . .

Guilt rose up, guilt he could not force away. Along with it came an unfamiliar feeling of concern for a woman he barely knew. Whatever their relationship, Tessa would not want harm to come to her sister. He owed Paige Hanner nothing, but he owed Tessa everything. If he just let Slade come for her . . .

Perhaps if he could make her leave before Slade came, go back to Colorado and forget whatever foolish notion she had in mind. Tell her he would do whatever she wanted him to do, but he would only do it alone. Then he could wait for Slade on his own.

His gaze went to the teepee and the reason he'd told himself he'd come here. The past was in there. And he would need the past when Slade came for him.

As if of their own volition, his legs carried him to the teepee, and he threw back the flap, then stepped inside. Within was only the blanket he slept on and his gunbelt, the one he had not strapped on since the day Tessa died. He knelt, lifting the belt, and the Peacemaker holstered within. As he drew the gun, his hand trembled but the cold steel felt somehow familiar and comforting. Hell, could he ever shoot straight anymore? He used to be fast, accurate. How much of that skill remained, buried beneath layers of guilt and whiskey?

It didn't matter. For if he were going to die when Slade came for him, he was going to do his damnedest to take the bastard with him.

★   ★   ★

Paige stepped from the marshal's office, confusion plaguing her mind and feelings for Teel Barsom stirring within her. She stood on the boardwalk, peering into the street, but not really seeing it, face grim. Was Betts right? Had she become attached to Barsom that quickly?

Betts thought him a coward, but the marshal simply didn't understand the drive to protect one's loved ones from danger. He was a man who'd never married, had no offspring or much to care about other than himself. And he was afraid of Heath; that was all too obvious.

She hadn't anticipated caring about her half-sister's husband. She hadn't expected even to like him. He was to be an instrument of vengeance and a tool to alleviate her guilt. She had blamed him, same as the marshal, for Tessa's death, until she saw what was in his eyes. She knew now; Tessa's death was not his fault in any way. And she felt . . . *something* for him. Something that might be wrong to feel. Something she had not felt for any man.

'You fool.' she told herself. 'Forgive me for that, too, Tessa.'

But it did not change that fact that Heath now knew something was going on. Her own fault. She hadn't figured on Heath's men being at the saloon taunting Barsom the very night she'd made her move with the marshal. Bad luck. Nor would she have expected the likes of those two half-wits to bother following her. She'd underestimated them.

She could not afford any further mistakes, or let her desire for vengeance cloud her thinking.

She sighed and began walking across the boardwalk. She'd left her horse in the alley next to the marshal's office. After taking the three steps to the hardpacked street, she went towards the alley.

Maybe vengeance wasn't the right word anymore. Maybe it had never been. Maybe the word was 'justice'. Justice for Tessa, for herself and for Barsom. Heath had to pay for his crimes; the marshal was right, and she knew it, and pay for them by bullet or by rope. But how could she prove he had killed her sister? Bring him in before Betts, Teel, or she ended up in the ground? She had precious little before Heath came after them, so maybe the question was moot. She no longer even had time to go through with her original plan, had she wanted to.

Whatever the case, she was going to tell Barsom the truth. He would leave, of course, and she would be on her own, but she would not run from Heath. She owed Tessa that much. And maybe she could kill him herself, not risk Barsom's life.

Tessa would not want that man hurt . . .

No, she wouldn't. And now Paige didn't, either. A man she had started out believing could be sacrificed for poor judgment was now one she felt a growing need to protect.

She came around the corner into the alley, her mind barely aware of her horse in front of her while she searched her thoughts for a way to trap Heath quickly. She saw none. The man hadn't survived unscathed this long without wits, but perhaps one of his men —

'Ma'am.' a voice came, startling her from her reverie.

He stood leaning against the opposite wall, a whiskey bottle in his hand, the outlaw called Jep, one of Heath's men.

Her hand darted into her riding skirt, came out with the derringer and brought it to aim on his chest.

The outlaw didn't move, merely stood staring at her, no emotion on his face.

'You don't need that,' Jep said. 'I ain't here to hurt you.'

'What do you want?' Her aim didn't

waver, though she fought to keep her hand from shaking. She was forced to admit, the times she'd rehearsed the confrontation with Heath and his men in her mind were considerably different from the reality of it. As often as she dreamed of putting a bullet in one of them, the thought of actually pulling the trigger gave her a chill inside.

'Heath sent me out to fetch a bottle.' He held up the whiskey. 'I saw you ride in and decided to wait till you came out of the marshal's.'

'I'll kill you,' she said, voice showing far more confidence than she felt.

'No, ma'am, you won't. You're not a cold-blooded killer. Don't become one now.'

'I ask you again, you sonofabitch, what do you want?'

A flush of crimson invaded his cheeks and a glint of anger sparked in his eyes, but he remained still.

'I'm a bad man, ma'am. I've done some bad things.'

'That ain't news. You ride with

Heath. Just because you ain't paid for your crimes don't mean you ain't done them.'

He nodded. 'I don't know who you are or what you got in mind for Barsom, ma'am. I can only assume Slade or one of us wronged you at some point and you're lookin' to get even. But I'm here to tell you you're ridin' the wrong trail.'

She cocked her head, studied him. If she had to say so, she guessed he was being sincere, warning her away for some reason. But why? He rode with Heath.

'Your name's Jep,' she said.

He nodded. 'You know that, you must have good reason to hate us.'

'I've got all the reason a person needs. You here to threaten me off? Ain't like Heath to do that, from what I hear tell. He's the type to strike without warning and not in the middle of town.'

Jep frowned. 'You're right. He is and he will. He knows you got Barsom out there and he's plannin' on takin' care of

you both. Soon. He was always plannin'
to finish with Barsom after he got done
enjoyin' watchin' the kid finish himself
with booze.'

'Why are you tellin' me this?' Suspicion flared in her eyes. She didn't trust
Heath or any of his men for a minute,
but something in the man's tone and
unwavering set of his eyes rang true.

'I'm tellin' you so you can leave. Ride
out in secret and go some place where
Heath will never find you. Take Barsom
with you.'

'And the marshal? Heath going to
come for him, too?'

The outlaw's head lowered, came
back up a moment later. 'You can't save
him. He's just a lawdog anyway.'

'Your concern overwhelms me.' She
put ice in her voice, but the derringer
came down, though she kept it ready
just in case he made a move.

'Concern? I ain't got a lick of it.
Regret . . . I got some of that. Hate? I
got a bellyful, but lucky for you it's all
for one man at the moment.'

'Who?'

He pushed himself away from the wall, a grin spreading across his lips. He walked from the alley and she kept her gaze riveted to him, half expecting Heath and the rest to spring around the corner and finish her off.

But they did not, and she let out a breath of relief.

She pocketed the derringer and mounted, then rode from the alley. She didn't know what Slade's man was up to, but it didn't make any difference. Any decision rested on her shoulders, and Teel Barsom's.

She hoped this time they made the right one.

11

By the time Teel Barsom reached the cabin, melancholy rode with him. It was a rare occasion when he returned to his camp sober, and the feeling was not one he cottoned to. Facing pain was something he'd spent his life avoiding. His folks had died when he was too young to recollect them, killed by outlaws in a stage hold-up. Those bandits had left him, a child of three or four, alive for some reason he would never know. He'd grown up in a series of homes, all his life holding on to a hatred of outlaws and the need to bring them to justice. But things had changed the day he met Tessa. The need to keep pursuing men like those who had killed his parents had abated that day. She had given him something more than a cause to pursue, an endless stream of wanted men to bring down.

But Slade Heath . . . Slade Heath he wished dead, the old motivations for being a manhunter returning with his sobriety.

Melancholy increasing, he reined to a halt, dismounted, then led the pinto into the barn. The sun was now touching the horizon, a blaze of red that splashed the grasslands with blood and shadow.

Again the craving for whiskey seared through his veins. He was usually at the saloon by this time, staring into a bottle of rotgut, and he wondered again why he had not gone directly there after Paige left, instead of to his camp, then back here. Maybe if he had just one to steady his nerves he'd be better prepared to handle Slade when he showed up.

You're lying to youself . . .

Would it be one drink? And it would it help in facing Slade? Or would he just end up the way he did each night?

He paused just short of the barn doors, gaze going to the trapdoor in the floor secured by the padlock. The whiskey was in there, Paige had told him. Had she taken the key with her? Left it in the house?

You're making another mistake . . .

Returning to the cabin, the need for whiskey strengthening with each step, he climbed the stairs and went to the door, opened it.

Just one wouldn't hurt, he told himself, sweat beading on his brow and a case of the shakes working through his body.

Once in the house, he paused, gaze roving. If she had left a key, where would she leave it? Surely not in the parlor or kitchen where he would likely be able to find it.

Her bedroom. His attention shifted to the closed door. If it weren't on her person, it would be in there. It had to be.

Don't do this . . .

As if his legs had a mind of their own, he went to the door, opened it, and looked into the room. It was small, sparsely furnished, with a bed, a small dresser holding a porcelain wash basin and pitcher, and a hardbacked chair over which was draped clothing, a dress, skirt, blouses. Powder-blue curtains hung on the window.

The room gave him the impression of someone who did not intend to stay, certainly not a woman planning on living here more than a short time, despite the garden. Or perhaps a woman who knew the reason that kept her here might kill her. The room seemed empty of most personal things, too, with the exception of a hairbrush and tintype resting on the dresser.

He went to it, picked it up. The picture was of two adolescent girls, both smiling, arms around each other. Tessa and Paige. Emotion balled in his throat and he swallowed, trying to force it away. With trembling fingers he touched the surface of the tintype. Loneliness rose inside him, deep and tormenting. How had his life come to this? How could Fate step in so callously? Christ on a crutch, he wished he knew. After long moments, he set the picture back on the dresser, lay it face down.

Beside the tintype lay a key.

She had left it in plain sight. He had no assurance this was the key to the padlock in the barn, but he had a notion it was and that it had been left there on purpose. The question was, why?

He picked up the key, turned it over in his hand, then closed his fingers about it. Backing out of the room, he shut the door, stood still, mind wandering through memories: Tessa laughing, her lips on his, her touch on his skin. The sensations came so powerfully it was almost as if she stood there before him.

But Slade Heath had made that impossible.

In a daze, he wandered from the cabin. By the time he reached the barn, sweat had formed on his brow and his mouth felt parched. The ride out to his former ranch and the tintype brought a flood of images to his mind. He kept seeing Tessa's face, then the smoldering remains of their home on that day eleven months ago. A memory staggered his step; he saw himself lifting the charred beam that day, and felt the wave of horror shuddering through him as if he were living it all over again. Her hand, flesh blackened, lay beneath the beam.

His memory grew hazy past that point, bloated with surges of pain and loss. He'd burned his hands pulling the beams off her, freeing her body from the wreckage. Wailing, he'd held her body in his arms, until the day turned to night, then to day again. He wasn't even sure how he'd managed to bury her, but he had found a shovel that had not been consumed by flames in the burned debris of the shed. He couldn't recall removing the ring from her finger, but somehow he had.

She would not want this. She wouldn't want you to suffer this way, to torture yourself. You have a second chance. Don't throw it away . . .

He dropped to his knees, shoved the key into the lock, tears blurring his eyes, memories of that day burning through his soul. The key turned, and the lock came open. With trembling fingers he tossed the lock aside, and he lifted the trapdoor. Beneath was an earthen compartment roughly three feet by two, maybe two deep. A bottle rested within.

He clutched the bottle, held it up. It was unopened, and it occurred to him it had been purchased relatively recently.

He stared into the amber liquor. He was deluding himself if he thought the whiskey would stop the pain, the memories, the loss. It would not. It was just a way of hiding, running from the mistakes he had made. If he took a drink now, he would not stop, and he would be a dead man when Slade came.

'Christamighty . . . ' he muttered. If Tessa could see him this way she'd be ashamed. She would forgive him anything he had done that day to save her, but she would not forgive him killing himself and letting her sister come to harm.

With a trembling sigh, he set the bottle back into the compartment, though every fiber of his being wanted to open it, drink down the whiskey until he could feel nothing. He'd spent such a long spell that way, he realized, he had not been able to think straight about Slade. If he let Slade find him drunk and kill him, he would be doing the same thing he had the day he'd given in and let the outlaw walk free: he would be condemning more innocent folks to death.

Paige Hanner, no matter her motives, had given him a chance. He would take it. If he were going to die, he would do it on his feet.

With a final glance at the bottle, he eased the trap-door shut, then relocked the padlock and stood, gazing down at the door. Face grim, he took a deep breath, then turned.

Paige Hanner stood in the barn doorway, one hand holding the reins to the big bay, the other on her hip. He had not heard her come up. She stared at him, silent, face expressionless.

'You left that key there on purpose, didn't you?' he said. 'That bottle hasn't been touched. You buy it just for me?'

A fleeting smile touched on her lips. 'I ain't proud of the fact, but I had to know if you'd be any good to me.'

'So it was a test?'

Without answering, she led the bay into the barn and to its stall, then began to unsaddle the animal.

'You could call it that, I reckon,' she said at last, after she had taken care of her saddle. 'But the choice was still yours.'

'What if I had failed?'

She closed the stall door, came up to him, her eyes locking with his. 'Then you'd have failed. You'd be right where I found you.'

'Except now Slade Heath would have a more pressing reason to kill me and an easier target.'

'We both know that was only a matter of time.'

'But you've endangered yourself. That, you didn't have to do.'

She looked down, folded her arms across her chest. 'I didn't expect to be followed. I knew sooner or later Heath would get wind of what I was doing, but I thought I'd have more time.'

'Then I think it's about time you told me what you *are* doing.'

Her head came up, eyes locking with his. 'When I heard from the marshal what happened to Tessa all I could think about was wanting Slade Heath dead. I couldn't do it myself.'

'You wanted me to kill him?'

'Who better? I didn't quite expect your condition, but it was a complication I could deal with. I'd get you sobered up and make you want to go after Heath, put a bullet in him. You used to be a man-hunter. You'd killed men before and you had the best reason in the world to want him dead. He

148

murdered your wife.'

'Marshal in on it, too?'

She nodded. 'Betts figures you for a coward, since you let Slade walk out of his cell. He's scared of him, wants him to pay for his crimes and don't care if it's perfectly legal.'

It didn't surprise him. He had seen the look in Betts' eyes when the marshal encountered him in town. Disappointment, disgust, blame. All deserved, as far as Teel was concerned. 'And he doesn't care what happens to me as long as I take Slade with me. Same for you.'

She hesitated, her shoulders dropping as if a weight of guilt had fallen on them. 'I blamed you for what happened to my sister when I first found out. I figured if you got killed it was an acceptable loss to get revenge on that man for what he did. Maybe in some ways I'm still a coward, too, because I wanted you to do my job for me. But things have . . . changed.'

His eyes searched hers and something within them frightened him, partly because he recognized the same feeling stirring within himself.

'Changed how? Slade is going to come for me, and you. You wanted me to kill him; I will if he attacks. It don't matter if he takes me with him.'

She shook her head slowly, tears shimmering in her eyes. 'It matters to me, now, Mr Barsom. I can see that I was wrong about you and I was wrong letting my hatred of Heath come at the expense of my principles. I want Heath to pay, but I won't risk your life, now. I'm sorry I ever thought about taking you out of that saloon and setting you up to get yourself killed. Tessa wouldn't have wanted that, but I was too damn stubborn and hate-filled to see it.'

He should have been angry with her, but he wasn't. He understood how it felt to abandon your principles for someone you loved. 'You did me a favor. All this time I've been drinking, trying to escape, I should have been facing what happened, going after Heath myself, proving something against him. I could have used my skills to bring him down, but I chose to hide in my pity instead. Betts is right: I am a coward. But I won't be anymore. I made a mistake eleven months ago. I can't change what I did and what happened, but I aim to right it the best I can.'

A tear slipped from her eye. 'Maybe there's another choice. One of Heath's men, the one called Jep, he was waiting for me when I left the marshal's office. He told me to leave, take you with me, go someplace Heath would never find us.'

'One of Slade's men told you that? Why?' Surprise welded on to his features.

'I don't know. It don't make sense unless he's got something against Heath, now. But maybe he's right. Maybe we could just go someplace and — ' She stopped, as if realizing she was about to say something that might be stepping over a line. Her cheeks flushed crimson, and she averted her gaze.

'I'm not leaving. Not now. Somehow I'll find a way to get Slade a necktie party.'

She shook her head. 'He isn't going to wait that long and you know it.'

He nodded. 'Then when he comes, I'll do what I should have done eleven months ago. You . . . ride away. Go back to Colorado until things are over.'

'After I was willing to throw away your life, you're trying to save mine?' Her hands went to his upper arms, gripping them gently.

'You weren't risking anything more than I already have since Tessa died. Only difference now is I have a chance to fight back. I owe you thanks for that.'

'Please, I saw that man's eyes. There's nothing in them. He doesn't care about life and he *will* kill you. There isn't enough time.'

He pulled away from her, turned towards the barn entrance, gaze lifting to the land beyond them. 'All the more reason I have to stay and correct a mistake I made letting him out. But you don't have to. You can go.'

Her head lifted, chin coming forward a notch and determination steeling her features. 'There's nothing for me in Colorado. There's nothing for me anywhere. I'm not running if you aren't going with me.'

'You have to.'

'No. I'm good with a gun. I owe it to Tessa's memory to finish what I started if you're going to risk your life.'

He didn't like it, but the way she said it reminded him of Tessa and he knew nothing he could say would change her mind.

The only thing left to do was prepare for death.

12

By the time Teel Barsom reined up before the marshal's office in Coopersville dawn painted the sky in shades of rose and ginger. He sat atop the pinto a moment, breathing in the cool morning air. The sun glinted off troughs coated with a veneer of ice and frosted window panes, and his breath steamed out. It had been a long time since he'd seen the town in this way, sober. He couldn't even recollect a dawn in the past eleven months, including the winter ones where he'd stayed at a small boarding house that tolerated him staggering in late nights. He'd forgotten its beauty.

Nobody walked the streets yet, but he knew Betts slept in an upstairs room of his office and was always up with the sunrise, though he rarely had anyone in his cells other than drunks sleeping off their whiskey.

Teel dismounted, every muscle pain-
ing from wood chopping the previous
day, but strangely it felt good. He
hadn't thought he could face a dawn
without Tessa, but he'd been wrong. It
stung, and grief had threatened to
overwhelm him numerous times on the
ride into town, but before Slade Heath
made a move, he had something he
needed to do, something he should
have done a long time ago.

He tied the reins to a hitch post,
climbed the steps to the boardwalk, and
went to the marshal's door. His belly
tightened as he tried the handle. It was
unlocked. As he expected, the marshal
was up. The lawdog stood before a
small wall mirror, drawing a razor over
his chin, as Teel entered. The scent of
coffee wafted from a blue enameled pot
on a small table. He didn't recollect
coffee smelling that good, but this
morning his senses seemed sharper
than they had been for a long while.

The marshal, a towel draped over his
shoulders, stopped shaving, damn near

dropping his razor as his gaze settled on Teel. Teel shut the door behind him.

'Betts . . . ' he said, with a slight nod.

'Jesus, Barsom,' the marshal said. 'You're the last person I expected to ever set foot in here again.'

'I reckon it's as much a surprise to me as it is to you. But I came to say something that needed saying eleven months ago.'

The marshal nodded, then wiped the remaining lather off his face and tossed the towel to a hard-backed chair. He went to the coffee pot, filled a tin cup. 'Offer you some?' He held out the cup. 'Or coffee ain't your drink.' The words came with an edge and Teel could see disapproval in the man's eyes.

Teel shook his head. 'I know you don't think much of me, Betts, and I reckon I can't blame you.'

Betts shrugged, went to his desk and sat, then took a sip of his coffee. He set the cup down. 'Some days I don't think much of myself, son. Maybe I shouldn't judge so much. Young woman made me

156

see I might be a stubborn old fool with my own fears.'

'That woman being Paige Hanner?' Teel stepped closer to the desk, gazed at the empty cells at the back. He had not been in the place since the day Slade Heath walked free and a chill slithered down his spine. He could still envision the outlaw sitting on the bunk, the dead look in his eyes.

The marshal nodded. 'One and the same. Pissed me off, too, but she was right when I thunk it over.'

'I'm aware of the feeling. She's got a way about her.'

'That she does. She's starting to fall in love with you, Barsom, you know that? She won't admit it to herself, yet, but I saw it in her eyes when she was here.'

The thought made Teel uncomfortable and he turned away from the marshal, went to the window and peered out into the brightening street. 'I know she wants me to kill Heath, and I know you've been going along with it.'

The marshal shifted in his chair, his turn to appear uncomfortable. 'Like I said, maybe I've had no call bein' so judgmental.'

'No, you had every call.' Teel turned to the marshal, leaned against the wall next to the window, and folded his arms. 'I let Slade Heath walk free eleven months ago. I lied to get him out.'

'I know.'

'His men threatened to kill Tessa if I didn't. I thought I was saving her life by doing what I knew was wrong. I'd do it again, if I thought it would bring her back. Heath's men, on his orders, I'm sure, killed her anyway. I was a fool thinkin' I could trust a man like that to keep his word.'

The marshal sighed. 'I'm an old man, son. I never married and never cared to. Didn't want to get attached to anyone in my line of work because I knew I'd make them a target. Least that's what I told myself. Fact is, I lied to myself all these years. I was just too damn scared to lose someone I might come to love. Thought about it a lot since Paige was here yesterday. I reckon I can't call you a coward without callin' myself one.'

'I aim to find a way to make Heath pay for what he did. I don't reckon he'll wait long before makin' a move on me or that young woman, but if I go out he's comin' with me. I just wanted to say I'm sorry for what I did last year, Marshal, before somethin' happens.'

'You don't owe me an apology — '

'I think I do. And one to all the folks Slade might have killed since he's been walkin' free. But it will be over soon, one way or another.'

The marshal's face carried a look of relief he couldn't hide. Paige was right: the man was scared Slade would come after him and wanted him dead or jailed before that happened.

'You're no coward. I was wrong, Barsom. I'm the one who owes you an apology.'

Teel gave him a grim smile, pushed himself away from the wall. 'Watch your back, Marshal. I reckon you know the reason.'

The lawdog nodded. 'I know.'

Teel paused, thoughts returning to Paige Hanner. 'How does she survive? Pay for the cabin?'

The marshal leaned back in his chair. 'From what she told me, her pa had himself a bit of money in the bank when he passed. He worked a mine, though he was a drunk. Somehow never missed a day on the job. They didn't get along, but he left it all to her after Tessa left. Won't last forever, though.'

Teel gave him a slight nod and went to the door. 'I don't come through this and Paige does . . . ' he glanced back at Betts, 'see to it she's taken care of. There's still some money in my account. Make sure she gets it.'

'Make her go, Teel. This is no place for her to be when Slade comes callin'.'

A grim smile filtered on to his lips. 'Had the same notion. I tried to make her go, but she refuses to leave.' With a departing nod to the lawdog, Teel opened the door and stepped out on to the board-walk. The sun had risen higher and the town was glazed with gold. People were starting to move about, heading towards the café or their shops.

'Well, well, lookee who's up bright and sober, Harris,' came a voice from the corner of the alley running next to the marshal's office.

Teel's gaze went to the man leaning against a wall there, a cigarette dangling from his lips. The one called Dickson. A second man stood close by, Harris.

Teel stepped off the boardwalk, knowing he was still not in any condition for a confrontation with those two. His lip was swollen from the fight at the saloon, and his body was stiff and sore. But it didn't matter. He was certain they were not going to kill him in the middle of town and risk being seen. That wasn't Slade's way.

'You stay the hell away from that cabin,' Teel said, stopping in front of Dickson.

Dickson smiled, let the cigarette drop

from his mouth. 'Well, you gone and grown yourself a new set since finding another woman, haven't ya, Barsom?'

Teel didn't even think about the move; it came without volition. Eleven months of pent up hate and fury overwhelmed him and he swung, surprised at how hard and fast his punch came. It took the outlaw in the jaw, buckled his legs.

Harris suddenly tried to grab him from behind, but Teel was ready for it this time. He pivoted, balance not as good as it could have been but adequate enough for the outlaw, who did not expect a drunk to be much of a problem. His elbow came up and snapped out, catching the man in the teeth. Harris uttered a squawk and blood sprayed from his mashed lips.

Dickson, partly recovered, swung a fist as Teel came back around. He tried to duck, but was rustier than he hoped and the punch caught him in the jaw, sent him staggering. Dickson uttered a cackle and lunged, swinging again.

Instinct took over, and Teel got under the blow, came up with an uppercut that clacked the outlaw's teeth together and knocked him backward, to slam into the wall. Mostly, it was surprise that gave Teel the advantage. Neither man had expected him to swing in the first place, or be any good at fighting in the second. Had they been ready things might have gone differently.

Harris slammed into Teel from behind, but Teel managed to twist, hit the wall with his back as the hardcase stepped in to finish the job. He jerked up his knee, burying it in the man's crotch, and Harris blew out a spittle-flecked grunt. The outlaw collapsed, curling into a ball in the dirt, groaning.

Teel spun, grabbed two handfuls of a dazed Dickson's shirt and slammed him into the wall. Pressing his face close, he said, 'You tell that sorry bastard you work for, not this time! Not. This. Time.'

He dropped the man, wiped blood from his own lip and left them in the alley. He wished right then and there he was the cold-blood killer Slade Heath was, because he would have put lead in both those men. But he was not. And he knew they would not draw on him. Not yet. With crashing certainty, he also knew he had made another mistake, letting his hate and anger get the better of him. He had given them fair warning he was not going to make himself the easy drunk target he had been for eleven months. And Slade would take advantage of that knowledge in some way.

★   ★   ★

'What the hell happened to you two?' Slade Heath asked as Dickson and Harris stumbled into the hotel room. Blood snaked from both men's lips and bruises swelled on their faces. Dirt covered their clothing.

Dickson glanced at Harris, who peered at the floor. Jep looked up from the table at which he was sitting, shuffling a deck of cards, a blank expression on his face. Slade, sitting in a chair near the window, rose to his feet and faced the two.

'Barsom happened,' Dickson said, voice low.

Slade didn't like that at all and it showed on his face. 'What do you mean, Barsom happened? You got beat up by a drunk?'

''Cept he wasn't drunk.' Harris tossed his hat on the bed then went to the table and collapsed on to a chair. Sunlight streamed in through the hotel window, cleaving a dusty arc over the table and worn carpet.

'Harris is right,' Dickson said. 'He was cold sober and we didn't expect him to just up and start swinging. Thought he was a coward.'

It was worse than Slade had thought. Somehow that woman had sewn some balls back on the boy and the fight would only add to his returning confidence. 'Where'd you run into him?'

'We was just gettin' done with some whores,' Dickson said. 'Saw him go into the marshal's office, so we decided to wait till he came out.'

'Anyone see you with him?' Slade pulled his chair to the table, lowered himself back on to it, then pulled a pack of papers from his shirt pocket.

Dickson shook his head, and with the back of his hand wiped a dribble of blood from the corner of his mouth. 'No one out that time of the morning. Was just plannin' on tryin' to find out who that woman is, but he just went loco and attacked us.'

Dickson was lying; Slade could tell. People were out on the street, however few, and someone might have seen the fight, but he reckoned it didn't matter. He fished a pouch from his pocket, then shook tobacco on to a slip of paper. After returning the pouch to his pocket, he rolled the paper, licked the edge and sealed it. 'That's goddamn bad news, Dickson,' he said, voice hardened, eyes locking on his man. Dickson backed up a step, his expression saying he half-expected to eat a bullet in the next moment. As much as Slade would have liked to accommodate him, he needed the man for the time being, at least until Barsom, the marshal and that girl were taken care of.

'We didn't think he was sober,' Dickson said. 'He never is.'

'You ever seen him wander around town that time of the morning, Dickson? Ever see him come out of the marshal's office in the entire eleven months since you killed his woman?' After locating a match in the pocket with the papers, Slade Heath struck it to light on a tooth, then lit the end of the cigarette.

Dickson shook his head, shifted his feet. 'No, not that I recollect.'

Slade uttered a humorless chuckle. 'Not that you recollect. You had half an ounce of smarts, you would have figured out Barsom was different.'

Dickson's face reddened with the insult and Slade cast him a look that challenged the outlaw to do something about it, but Dickson didn't make a move. He knew better. Slade respected that. Dickson was too stupid and too scared of him to try anything. Unlike Jep, whom he still suspected needed watching.

'We didn't think about that,' Dickson said.

'Just what did you think about, Dickson?' Slade took a drag from his cigarette, let the smoke trickle out, his gaze never moving from the outlaw. The scar on his face seemed unnaturally white in the sunlight streaming through the window that washed over the side of his face.

'Like I said, maybe we could get him to tell us who that woman was.'

'Right there in the middle of town? Reckon you know my policy where witnesses are concerned. If someone of note saw you go after him there'd be a link to us when we killed him. I don't like links, Dickson.'

Beads of sweat formed on the outlaw's forehead, ran from his brow. His face bleached from red to gray.

'No one saw us.'

'No one?' Slade's brow arched.

Dickson went a shade paler. 'Was only a few folks on the street. No one paid us any mind. They're afeared of us.'

'You best be right . . . ' The threat flashing in Slade's eyes was clear.

'Won't happen again, Slade, I swear.'

He was goddamned right about that, Slade thought. Because once he got rid of Barsom and the girl, he would be leaving town without Dickson. The jury was still out on Harris and Jep.

'See to it it don't.' Slade took another drag, irritation crawling through his nerves. Barsom sober was the exact problem he did not want. Somehow that woman had turned him around in a very short space of time and now he was a danger. And that danger would increase by the day.

Just who the hell was she? Why did she want that boy sober? To kill Slade or bring him to justice? That meant he had wronged her somewhere along the way and she wanted revenge, and planned to use Barsom to get it. It didn't matter to him what the act had been, how he had incurred her wrath, only that now she needed to be dealt with before she could bring Barsom any further along. If Slade waited for the boy to find his skills again, things might go the wrong way, despite the advantage in men.

'We move tonight,' Slade said after a few moments. Dickson had not budged but now seemed to relax a mite.

'Tonight?' Jep said, looking up from his cards.

Slade glanced at him. 'You got objections to that?'

Jep's face tightened. Balls of muscles stood out to either side of his jaw. 'No . . . ' he said, voice low.

'You best not. And you best get your bottles together because that gal's going to have the same accident Barsom's wife had. I want that cabin and barn burnt to the ground.'

A look flashed across Jep's face,

quickly gone, and Slade expected the man to say something, but he remained silent. If Jep failed in his duty, there'd be a third body found in the torched ruins of the cabin.

'What about the marshal?' Dickson asked, finally moving from his spot and going to a chair, apparently figuring out he was not going to be shot on the spot.

Slade shrugged, took another drag on his cigarette, then mashed it out on the table top. 'Marshal's old. He's about to retire.'

13

Teel Barsom drew his Peacemaker and triggered a shot at the whiskey bottle he'd taken from the barn. The bottle sat in the center of old bean cans lined up on the fence at the north edge of the property he'd repaired earlier in the day. The shot thundered in the afternoon air and the recoil kicked his arm back a bit more than he expected, causing the shot to miss by quite a bit.

He was indeed rusty. The gun had come out of the holster slower by fractions, but in manhunting fractions mattered — they meant the difference between life and death. And in the case of Slade Heath they meant utter failure and the life of that young woman at the cabin.

The acrid scent of blue-gray gunsmoke assailed his nostrils and he holstered the weapon, staring at the bottle and cans on the fence, doubts swimming in his mind. Even after a year of drunkenness he should have hit one of them. That he didn't brought a measure of discouragement, along with a surge of frustration. He would not get the drop on Slade or his men with his shooting, that was for sure.

'Damnit . . . ' he muttered.

The day was waning, the sun heading towards the low hills, and while the grounds looked peaceful now, they would not appear that way for long; Teel felt certain of it. Time had run out, especially after this morning's encounter outside the marshal's office.

He drew a deep breath of cool air, tried to force himself to relax, though he'd still experienced off and on bouts of those damnable shakes. He wondered many a time since placing the bottle on the fence whether he'd be better off drinking it than shooting at it.

His hand swept for his gun. The Peacemaker came up, blasted. The move felt a bit smoother this time, more natural. But he still missed.

'Christ on a crutch!' he said, voice like a whip.

A shot thundered behind him and he nearly came out of his skin. One of the cans jumped off the fence as a bullet punched through it.

He spun, his gun still in his hand, to find Paige standing ten feet behind him, the Winchester braced against her shoulder, gaze sighting down the barrel. She lowered the rifle and that annoying smirk came back to her full lips.

'Very funny,' he said, not at all amused.

She laughed, the first easy emotion he'd heard from her in the past two days. 'That's how it's done, Mr Barsom. Told you I could shoot.'

He frowned, holstered his gun. 'Appears the year took its toll on my aim.'

'Keep practicing. It'll come back.'

'I've run out of time. After what happened this morning, Slade will move faster. He knows now I'm sober and he won't let me have time to regain my skills completely. I made another mistake, Paige. I tipped my hand because I let my temper get the better of me.'

She came up beside him, sighted down the barrel and pulled the trigger. Another can jumped from the fence.

'So? Let him come.' She tried to sound confident but he could hear in her voice she wasn't. Fear peered from her eyes, but if he had to guess it was not fear over her own safety; it was fear over his.

'I ain't ready. Slade is.'

She lowered the rifle, held it by the barrel and rested the stock on the ground. 'I don't want you to die, Teel. I know it's my fault I brought you here in the first place and I planned for revenge. But I ain't never met anyone like you. I know why Tessa loved you, I truly do. And I know I just met you but I want to give you a reason for goin' on, one that don't involve Slade Heath.'

He wasn't sure what she was saying,

but had a notion it had to do with what the marshal had said earlier. And he found it stirred things within him he would just as soon not have felt at that moment.

'Maybe you already have. I spent far too much time feelin' sorry for myself, not facing what I should have faced. I let Tessa down in more ways than just the choice I made that day she died. But I have to finish this with Slade before I can even think of going on. When you got here you might have wanted me to go after Slade, but I was runnin' from the fact I always wanted that, too. If I let him go again . . . you'll die this time, way Tessa did then. I won't have that on my conscience. I've got enough guilt already.'

She nodded, then suddenly stepped towards him, dropping the Winchester. She slid her arms around his waist, laid her head on his chest. He swallowed hard, his own arms coming up, wrapping around her. They stood there in silence long enough for the sun to jump handspan towards the low hills and shadows from the stands of cottonwoods that dotted the land to stretch towards them in weird shapeless patterns. At last she pulled back, stooped to pick up the rifle.

She didn't look at him, didn't say another word, merely started back to the house.

He turned towards the bottle, eyes narrowing on it. It would be tonight. He knew it. Slade would come. And he was not ready. But unlike that day with Tessa, he would be present when Death rode in, and do his best to protect the young woman. He could not think of the tomorrow beyond that, because there might not be one.

His hand swept to his Peacemaker again, drew. The move came much smoother this time.

But he still missed.

* * *

Marshal Betts had called Teel Barsom a coward to Paige Hanner, but who was he kidding? He knew who the real coward was and it wasn't that boy. Teel was just grief-stricken and had made stupid mistakes; a real coward would have run — the way Betts planned to.

The marshal walked along the boardwalk towards his office. The sun had set an hour ago and a few cowboys sauntered along the street, heading for the saloon after a day tending herd. They laughed, joked, unaware of the danger that lurked in the town, though that danger didn't directly threaten them at the moment. They were the lucky ones.

The danger threatened Barsom and Paige, and himself. Paige had been right when she had accused him indirectly of being afraid of Heath. He was. He always had been and he reckoned he had good reason. He'd held that man in a cell, been nervous about it the whole time and, truth be told, he had hoped that damned outlaw would spend the rest of his life behind bars. He had arranged it with the town council, who would try the man, to put him away for a long spell. If he had been able, he would have seen him hanged, but the council had not wanted to go quite that far. Despite knowing Heath was responsible for numerous hold-ups and killings in the area, no one had a lick of proof or a witness and having to justify the hanging to the county law might have been a problem.

But the day Barsom had brought Heath in, Betts had looked into the eyes of that sonofabitch and seen a monster. He'd never seen a dead man living, but Heath was damn sure one. And Betts had known the moment Barsom forced the release that neither of their lives were worth a wooden nickel. But it had been a simmering thing, an event for the future, because Slade Heath had been enjoying Barsom's fall into the bottle. Now things were different. Paige had sobered up the boy and made a mistake. Two mistakes, actually, he reckoned. The first had been in picking the wrong night to haul Barsom out of the saloon, when two of Heath's men were there. He supposed that was partially his fault, too. He had helped, and should have figured out a better place to take Barsom, but the kid spent his time only in two places — the saloon and at the camp he'd made on his land. Betts had gotten too eager, practically rejoiced the night Paige came in to tell him she was making her move.

Her second mistake was in starting to fall for Barsom. He had seen it clearly in her eyes, even if she didn't realize it herself. She was falling in love with that boy, the same way her sister had. And that made her not want to follow through with her plan, not risk his life. The problem was, with Heath knowing about her and Barsom being out at her cabin, she was left with no choice but to risk it, now, as well as her own. Or run.

That's what Betts was going to do. He'd decided it this morning when Barsom paid him the visit. Though he hadn't said anything, he'd felt shame for accusing the boy of being a coward, because one look at him today told him that was not the truth. The truth was, the coward had been staring back at him from the shaving mirror.

Heath would not give them time to get Barsom ready. They knew it and Betts knew it, and he wanted to live. He wasn't a particularly young man, but he had a few years left and he wanted to keep them. Heath was going to come for him first, he felt certain, and he reckoned it would be within the next few days. That meant he had to ride out tonight, vanish from Coopersville until he got word Heath had been taken in or killed. If that word never came, Betts would know Barsom and Paige were dead, and he would never go back.

The thought of running made him feel like a lowly sonofabitch, but, hell, he was too damn old for gun-fights and outlaws like Slade, and those two had no chance, even if he rode out there to the cabin to help.

He shook his head, disgusted with

himself, but what could he do? If he could take comfort in one thing, it was that he had stopped at the telegraph office earlier and sent a message to the county marshal, telling him Slade was going on a rampage and was planning to attack Barsom. They would send men. He prayed it would not be too late.

Marshal Betts suddenly stopped, glanced behind him. Had he heard a noise? Of course he had. Men were out on the boardwalk. He was just antsy, imagining things. He'd seen no sign of Heath or his men. He shivered as a chill snaked down his spine. He wasn't sure if it was from anxiousness or guilt, but supposed it made no difference.

'I'm sorry, Barsom,' he mumbled, starting forward again. 'I didn't understand what you did but I should have. I'm doing much worse.'

Reaching his office, he fished in his pocket for a key. A dry leaf skittered along the boards, blown by a gust of chilled autumn air, and he jumped, despite himself. His gaze swept backward, but again he saw no one but those who belonged there. He kicked at the leaf, then inserted the key into the lock. The click it made turning sounded as loud as a gunshot to him, and he shuddered again.

Hell, he wasn't usually this jittery, even about Heath, but he reckoned all the thinking he'd done about the outlaw, and his burning guilt over leaving Barsom and Paige, had set him more on edge.

He opened the door, stepped into the darkened office. Closing it behind him, he stood in the dark a moment, then went to the small table and fired the lantern. He kept the flame low, so it wouldn't reach beyond the office and possibly attract Heath or one of his men, though he felt fairly certain they would not attack him here, where someone might see. He moved to the coffee pot, poured himself a cup of cold Arbuckle's and swallowed it in one long drink, wishing it was something a mite stronger.

He set the cup down, and his fingers went to the tin star at his breast. He plucked it from his chest, suddenly hurled it at the wall. It clinked as it rebounded to the floor.

'You don't deserve to wear that anymore,' he told himself. 'Cowards don't get to wear badges.'

'Crisis of faith, Marshal?' a voice came from behind him and he let out a gasp, swore he came a foot off the floor.

He spun, to see a shadowy figure sitting in the chair behind his desk. Oh, Christ. He had made a mistake. His last, he reckoned. For in that chair sat Slade Heath, a gun in his hand, aimed square at his chest.

'Heath . . . ' he said, barely getting the word out. His tongue didn't want to work right and his throat constricted, smothering his voice.

'Come now, Marshal Betts,' Heath said, swinging his feet off he desk and standing. 'Surely you knew I'd come.'

'I . . . I knew.' Betts didn't move. He couldn't. Every muscle seemed frozen.

He could not draw on the man, because Heath was holding a gun on him, but doubted he could have even if that were not the case. He'd never had to draw on anyone and was not in the same category of quickness Barsom was by a long shot.

'Didn't think it would be so soon, though, did you?' Slade Heath laughed, the sound echoey and chilling in the low light of the room. 'Truth to tell, I didn't, either, but your friends made it necessary. See, after I'm done with you, we're going to pay them a visit, then move on. I'm sure you'll be glad to know we'll be leavin' your fine little town, though the information won't do you much good.'

'Please . . . ' Betts said, struggling to get the word out.

'Well, there's something I didn't think I'd see: the marshal beggin'. And beggin' for himself, not his friends. Reckon I thought that boy was pathetic, wallowing in his grief, drinkin' away his life, but you're worse, Betts.'

185

Slade Heath was right. Betts knew it. But right then he would have done anything to save his life and it disgusted him. 'Don't do this, Heath. Just leave. Nobody here's got anything on you. You done enough to that boy. You took everything he had.'

Slade Heath came around the desk, moved closer to the marshal. 'See, I know that, Betts. Truly, I do. But you and him put me in a cell like some kind of animal and I just can't let that go. What can I say, I hold a grudge.' Heath drew back the hammer of his Smith & Wesson, gestured towards the cell he had once occupied. 'In there.'

Betts licked his lips, could barely make his legs move, but complied. Slade Heath followed him in.

'Bet you were thinkin' you were safe, seein' as how you know I don't like takin' chances on gettin' caught and we're right in the middle of town, the marshal's office, no less. And you're right, least partially. It were daytime I wouldn't be tryin' this.'

186

'Someone will hear the shot, Heath,' Betts said, mustering a last surge of defiance.

'A truism, surely.' Heath edged around Betts, grabbed the blanket from the bunk. With one hand, he balled it up, keeping the gun on the marshal with the other.

Horror washed over the marshal's face. Slade Heath smiled, the scar wriggling in the low light like a demon snake.

The outlaw jammed the gun into the wadded blanket and pulled the trigger.

A hole appeared in Betts' shirt and a death mask froze on his face. He was conscious for a moment of deep searing pain and warm fluid pumping from the wound, soaking his shirt. He dropped, blackness sweeping in from the corners of his mind. A moment later he felt nothing more.

* * *

Slade Heath stared down at the body of Marshal Betts, satisfaction running through his veins. He'd wanted to do that for a very long time, and seeing the fear in the man's eyes and hearing him beg had not been a disappointment.

He went to the door near the back, next to stairs that led up to the marshal's sleeping quarters. He opened it, having destroyed the lock an hour ago when he broke in. A sharp whistle brought shapes out of the darkness. His men filed into the office and Slade holstered his gun.

'He's in the cell.' He ducked his chin at Dickson and Harris. 'You two get rid of the body some place no one will ever find it, then meet me and Jep back at the livery. Jep, go on to the livery, now, get your horse and make sure you get your bottles in your saddle-bags. Make sure no one sees you.'

Jep frowned in the dim light and Slade wondered if he wasn't trusting the man too far, but for the moment he didn't have much choice. He'd already made arrangements, however, with Dickson and Harris to have them kill Jep the moment Barsom and the girl were finished. Then Slade would take care of the other two and ride out alone. Earlier that afternoon, he'd spent some time moving their stash of gold, cash and jewelry to a place where only he would be able to find it.

Things were goin' right fine, he figured. They always went his way. No one would ever put him in a cell again; he was unstoppable. A small laugh came from his lips as his men carried out his orders. In a few hours he would move on to a whole new town and a whole new life, nobody left behind who could ever identify him. Including his own men.

14

With nightfall, Teel Barsom turned the lantern on the mantle in the parlor low, then checked the load in his Peacemaker. It was full, but would it matter if Slade Heath came charging in here tonight? If his luck hitting the damned whiskey bottle was any indication, it wouldn't. He slapped the gate closed, holstered the weapon, mouth drawn into a grim line.

Paige had taken the Winchester down from above the fireplace and set it against the couch. Lines of worry deepened on her face as she gazed at him.

'Maybe he won't come tonight and we'll have more time,' she said.

He shook his head, moving to one of the front windows. 'He'll come. After that fight I had with his men, he won't give me time to get my feet set.'

He peered out into the moon-streaked

night, eyes narrowing, searching for any signs of life. Alabaster light fell over the grasslands, blending with shadows cast from cottonwoods. A chilled breeze rustled the leaves and blades of browning grass, but nothing else stirred.

'Maybe we should get the marshal out here, even the odds.' Paige moved to another window, looked out.

'Betts is an old man. He's got a right to be scared, I reckon, but a scared man, even a lawman, might do us more harm than good right now.'

Moments dragged into an hour, then two. The moon jumped a handspan across the black-velvet sky studded with diamond stars. Teel's nerves started to crawl. The urge for a drink washed over him again, but not as severe this time. From the corner of his eye he looked at Paige, her face pale but her body rigid with courage. He couldn't deny the things he was starting to feel for her and the desire to protect her the way he had not been able to protect Tessa was growing. But it was far too late now to convince her to leave, and the point was moot because she was as stubborn as her half-sister.

'It's comin' up on midnight,' Paige said, with a glance at the small clock on the mantle. 'I don't like just sittin' here bein' a target.'

He nodded, expression remaining grim. 'I don't care a lick for it, either, but at least holed up we have a chance. Out in the open he'd have us — '

A sound from the distance stopped him dead. At first he wasn't sure his worried mind hadn't simply imagined it. But it grew louder, at first like drums echoing from a dream, then becoming the pounding of hoofs beating from a nightmare.

'Oh, hell . . . ' he said, easing up the window a foot so he would have an opening to shoot from. 'Horses.'

Paige nodded, fear flashing over her face, but quickly mixing with determination. She went to the couch, grabbed the Winchester and returned to her window. She lifted it a few inches, then

192

jammed the rifle barrel into the opening.

'I only see three of 'em,' she said a moment later.

He nodded. 'Slade's men, near as I can tell. Why ain't Slade with them?'

'Case they lose, maybe,' she said. 'Then the law can't blame Slade for something his men did.'

His brow furrowed. Under normal circumstances that might have been true, but he saw no way Slade would sit this out. And whatever else the outlaw was, he was no coward.

Thunder suddenly boomed across the yard and Paige's window shattered. She uttered a short scream as a bullet plowed through the glass, spraying her with shards.

Startled, she yanked the Winchester's trigger, returning fire, but without the benefit of aiming, and hit nothing.

More shots followed, a volley of them. The *thuk-thuk-thuk* of lead punching into the wood about the window was accompanied by more glass shattering as the window before Teel disintegrated.

He threw up a forearm, shielding his eyes from the flying slivers, pumping a shot out at the yard at the same time.

Bullets kept coming as the three riders branched off, attacking the front of the house from different angles.

A yelp came from Paige and she fell back. He swore his heart stopped, only starting again when she came back up to her knees. Blood swelled where lead had gouged a deep furrow across her blouse and left shoulder.

'I'm all right!' She crawled back to the window, still clutching her rifle.

He let out the breath he had been holding and jammed his Peacemaker through what was left of the window, now only pieces of frame. He fired two shots, aiming at the front man, who looked to be Dickson, but it was difficult to tell in the moonlight. He missed and let out a curse. A bullet drilled into the frame inches from his head, splintering wood.

'I can't hit them!' he said, a note of panic in his voice.

'You're thinkin' too much!' Paige yelled back at him over the crash of gunfire. 'Just shoot.' She pulled the trigger and one of the men jolted in the saddle. Harris, if Teel guessed right.

A return volley came immediately from the outlaws, lead whining into the house, burying itself in the floor and opposite wall.

Despite being hit, Harris fired back, riding his horse in a zigzagging pattern to avoid being struck again.

Where the hell was Slade? The thought thundered through Teel's mind as loud as the gunfire. He fired again, missing. Four more shots; four more misses. They did not have a chance unless they picked off two men right away. The house would not provide enough protection and the outlaws would be far better stocked with ammunition; they could keep up the attack until Teel and Paige ran out of bullets.

A chill suddenly snaked down his spine. The thought of his burned-out ranch rose in his mind. Jesus! If they lit the place on fire —

As if in answer, a sudden *whoosh*! sounded from somewhere outside and an orange glow fluttered across the grass.

His blood ran cold. They'd set something on fire, but it wasn't the house.

'The barn!' he said, realization dawning on him. But why the barn?

'What?' Paige pulled the trigger and Harris jolted out of his saddle. 'Oh, God . . . ' Her face went white and he knew the reality of actually shooting a man had come crashing home in her mind, despite the fact they were outlaws trying to kill them.

'The barn's on fire,' he said, triggering another shot at the marauding Dickson. 'Why didn't he set the house on fire?'

'Oh, my God, the horses!' Paige said and his belly plunged.

Bullets thudded into the house and another came through the paneless window, drilling into the couch. He popped the gate of his Peacemaker, reloaded with bullets from his gunbelt, slapped it shut.

Beyond the window the roar of flames grew louder and the yard brightened. A whoop came from Dickson as the outlaw sent more bullets drilling into the window frame and side of the house.

Teel drew a bead on the outlaw, fired. Dickson suddenly lifted out of his saddle, flew backward and slammed into the ground while his horse veered off and kept running. Dickson didn't move, his body strangely twisted.

'You hit him,' Paige said, a flash of relief on her face.

He shook his head. 'I don't think so.'

'But he's down.'

'I know.' Except for the roar of flames things went eerily quiet. He'd lost track of the other outlaw, Jep, didn't see him. Crawling away from the window, he moved towards the door.

'Where are you going?' Paige asked, hands bleached around the stock of her rifle.

'Stay in here. It's too quiet. Slade's up to something. I'm going after him. There's a cellar opening in the kitchen.

Get down in it and fire at anyone who tries opening the trapdoor.'

She shook her head, eyes flooding with worry. 'No, you can't go out there.'

'We've already lost the barn and two horses, I ain't gonna wait for him to fire the cabin.'

'Then I'll cover you.'

Teel glanced at her, saw there was no arguing. He didn't try. He edged the door open, keeping to the side of it and peering around the frame out at the porch. He spotted no sign of anyone and eased out, Peacemaker held ready at the side of his face. He might not be able to hit a bottle at fifty paces but he could sure as hell hit something a few feet in front of him. He pulled the door shut behind him, then crouched, scooted along the porch.

The barn was ablaze, great tongues of flame licking at the night sky and plumes of black smoke billowing into the night. The sight brought a horror-filled memory back to his mind of the day he'd found his ranch burned. A few hundred yards from the barn two horses bolted in the direction of town. The same two that had been in the barn.

'What the hell?' he whispered. Slade had released the horses before setting the barn on fire? Acts of kindness weren't like the outlaw. It made no sense. Something was wrong.

An instant later that thought crashed home; the outlaw named Jep stepped around the corner as Teel reached the end of the porch and shoved a gun into his face.

★ ★ ★

Paige Hanner had a piece of hope. Two of Slade's men were down; that left Jep and Slade himself. And Slade was nowhere to be seen. She shuddered. She had never killed a man before and she was sure having done so would give her nightmares if they came through this. But for the moment she couldn't dwell on it. They had far from escaped and Teel was out there alone.

She peered into the night, the orange flickering glow of flame light splashing across the yard. It looked like some vision straight out of Hell. A burst of sadness came for her horses but she suppressed that, too. She couldn't see Teel, assumed he was sneaking along the porch, but she kept her rifle ready, in case the one called Jep came into the open. Despite a sick knot in her belly from killing Harris, she would do it again to save Teel's life.

As she listened, only the roar of flames reached her ears. She heard nothing of Teel, but swore the sound of hoofbeats came in muffled beats, fading into the distance.

And a creak. She stiffened, the sound puzzling her. It was the sound of a boot stepping on old wood, and she tried to see along the porch. Was it Teel?

Then a chill went through her blood and her breath caught in her lungs. She tried to turn but something jammed against her temple, something cold, hard — the muzzle of a gun.

She froze, hands tightening on the rifle, forearms aching with the strain, knuckles bleaching bone white.

'A year ago,' came a voice near her ear, sending a shiver down her spine, 'I never would have gotten away with this. Manhunters have that damned sixth sense about things. Whiskey took more than just your man's dignity, didn't it?'

Paige eased her head around and gazed up at the leering face of Slade Heath and the piece of hope she had felt a moment before turned into a knell of doom.

★   ★   ★

Teel Barsom froze, expecting the sound of a gunshot to be the last thing he heard when Jep pulled the trigger and blew his face off. There was no way he could get his own gun to aim before the outlaw fired.

But the shot didn't come. Jep held a finger to his lips, then lowered his gun.

'You got one chance, Barsom, and

I'm it. But you have to agree to let me go free after.' The outlaw's voice came low, barely audible.

'You . . . you let the horses go?' Teel's eyes narrowed.

The outlaw, climbed up on to the porch, nodding. 'I killed Dickson, too, that brainless sonofabitch. But that don't matter. We best get back in the house 'cause Slade is already sneaking in the back by now. He had me light the fire to draw you out. He don't think much of your manhunting skills anymore.'

Teel's belly dropped. Slade was right. He should have thought about a lure. Another mistake, perhaps his last.

'Why should I trust you?' Teel said, but he was already straightening and moving back along the porch towards the door.

'Well, I could have shot you just now and frankly you ain't got a choice. I want Slade dead. Just remember you agreed to let me go on my way.'

Teel nodded. He didn't like it but saw no other option.

Teel reached the door, slid his hand around the handle, Jep behind him. Turning the knob, he fought a surge of panic that threatened to overwhelm him. Easing it open, he froze in the doorway.

Slade stood there in the middle of the room, one arm around Paige's waist, clamping her against him, the other hand pressing a Smith & Wesson to her temple. Her face was pale, her lip quivering, but he saw defiance in her eyes.

'Go, Teel!' she yelled. 'Run!'

'Oh, he won't run,' Slade Heath said, the scar wriggling in the low light as he spoke. 'His type only runs from their guilt, not a threat to their woman. That right, Barsom? Do come in and drop your gun.'

Teel took a step into the parlor, but held on to the gun. 'Let her go. You can kill me, but don't hurt her.'

'Why would I do that, Barsom? I have you both.' The outlaw's eyes held an utter lack of emotion. Death grinned like weathered skulls within them. Again, he had the advantage and he knew it. He always had it, and Teel just had not been ready for him. Now, Paige would pay for it, the way Tessa had.

'She ain't done nothing to you.' Teel couldn't see what had happened to Jep, but had the sense the outlaw was no longer behind him.

'On the contrary. She got you sober, made my life more difficult. Where's Jep? You kill him? I didn't hear a gunshot.'

Teel nodded, taking another step closer to the outlaw and Paige. He glimpsed movement from the kitchen, forced himself not to look, hoping the revelation didn't show in his eyes.

'You're all alone now, Slade. Give it up.' Teel suddenly knew he needed to keep Slade talking, cover any sound that might occur behind the outlaw. 'You've got no men left and if you shoot her I'll shoot you.'

Slade laughed, the sound shuddering through him. 'I'd just kill you first, Barsom, and you know it. 'Sides, was fixin' to retire my men, anyway. You did me a favor — '

Slade suddenly swung the gun backward and fired. Somehow he had picked up on Teel's trying to cover Jep's approach.

The sound of the shot was earshattering, the result startling and final. Any hope of Slade's man evening the odds was gone. A bullet punched into the outlaw's chest, sent him backward a step. The gun dropped from his nerveless fingers and he peered down at the blossoming blood rose on his shirt. His mouth came open, as if to speak, but only a snake of blood came out. An instant later, he collapsed.

Slade got no time to gloat over his victory this time. Seizing the opportunity Jep had given them, the gun momentarily away from her head, Paige stamped on Slade's instep and jammed an elbow back into Slade's breadbasket. Slade let out a yell and tried to bring the gun back around, but Paige dropped and Teel's gun came up.

The move was pure reflex, something inbred from years on the trail. This was no bottle he was shooting at; it was a man who was about to murder a young woman.

He fired. There was no chance of missing this time and the bullet drilled into Slade's shoulder, kicked him back. His gun flew from his fingers, hit the floor and spun away.

A roar came from Slade's lips and he lunged towards Teel. Teel could have fired but waited, timing Slade's lunge and snapping up the gun as the outlaw came in. The gate clacked from Slade's jaw, snapping his head back. He staggered, but held his feet. Teel swung the gun again, taking the outlaw in the temple. Slade collapsed, eyes going blank, hitting the floor face first.

Teel aimed the gun at the back of the outlaw's head, hand shaking. It would be so easy just to pull the trigger now, avenge Tessa.

A hand covered his, pressed the gun down. Head turning, he looked into Paige Hanner's blue eyes.

'I wanted him dead, too. But if you kill him this way, it'll make you no better than him. His bullet's in his man and he set the barn afire. There are witnesses this time. The council will have enough to link him to Tessa's murder and tryin' to kill us to put a rope around his neck. You ain't a cold-blooded killer, Teel. Tessa wouldn't want you to be.'

He nodded, wanting to pull the trigger and end the life of the man who'd caused so much pain, so much death. But, hand shaking, at last he lowered the gun. It was over. Slade would face the justice he'd escaped for so long.

That would have to be enough.

★   ★   ★

Teel Barsom knelt before the gravestone on his land, Tessa's ring in his hand. The morning sun coated the grasslands with gold and for the first time in a long time he felt almost a sense of peace come over him.

He pressed the ring deep into the soil, mouthed a silent prayer. Slade Heath was in jail under guard. Marshal

Betts had disappeared but when he and Paige had brought Slade in, they'd found the county marshal and two of his deputies searching for him. Teel could only assume Slade had killed the man and for that he felt truly saddened. In the end, Slade had made a mistake, too. He'd gotten cocky after years of avoiding the law, always winning. Paige had been right when she'd seen the outlaw's weakness. Still, the hardcase might have won, had it not been for his man turning on him. Maybe it was just a case of the outlaw's luck finally running out.

The sound of hoofs brought him from his thoughts and he looked up to see Paige approaching, having retrieved her bay and the pinto he'd ridden to town. She reined up, dismounted.

He stood, peered at her as she approached. 'How did you know where I'd be?'

She gave him a thin smile. 'You weren't at the cabin and like I said, I watched you for a spell. I knew where you stayed at night.'

He nodded. 'Just sayin' . . . good-bye . . . '

She looked down at the grave, a tear slipping from her eye. 'The county men found the marshal's body by the creek. Prairie wolves had dragged it out of some brush where Slade or his men hid it. They're sure it's Slade's bullet in him. He'll hang.'

'Better'n he deserves.'

She gazed at him, her eyes searching his. 'Where do you go from here, Mr Barsom?' Her voice came low, trembly, as if she were afraid of the answer.

'I won't be going back to the bottle. Manhunting, either. I thought about it a lot after we took Slade in. Tessa . . . she wouldn't want me going back to either. She'd want me to rebuild.' His hands came up, gripping Paige's upper arms and turning her towards him. 'I want you to help me. Can't run a ranch by myself and I think your sister would want you to stay, too.'

A smile fluttered on her lips, and he

could feel her body tremble. 'It don't feel wrong. I thought it would, but it don't.'

He nodded, then went back to the pinto and mounted, while she followed suit with her own horse.

'You know anything about longhorns?' he asked, giving her an arched brow.

'Know they're not as ornery and full of bull as some men.' She winked. 'I'll figure it out.'

'I got a notion you will.' He laughed and reined around, gigging the pinto into an easy gait, the feeling that Tessa was now at peace and granting them her approval riding with him.

THE END

We do hope that you have enjoyed reading this large print book.

Did you know that all of our titles are available for purchase?

We publish a wide range of high quality large print books including:
Romances, Mysteries, Classics
General Fiction
Non Fiction and Westerns

Special interest titles available in large print are:
The Little Oxford Dictionary
Music Book, Song Book
Hymn Book, Service Book

Also available from us courtesy of Oxford University Press:
Young Readers' Dictionary
(large print edition)
Young Readers' Thesaurus
(large print edition)

For further information or a free brochure, please contact us at:
Ulverscroft Large Print Books Ltd.,
The Green, Bradgate Road, Anstey,
Leicester, LE7 7FU, England.
Tel: (00 44) 0116 236 4325
Fax: (00 44) 0116 234 0205

Other titles in the
Linford Western Library:

LADY COLT

Steve Hayes

When word comes through that two of the infamous Wallace brothers have been spotted in Indian Territory, Liberty Mercer — only the second woman ever to become a Deputy US Marshal — rides out to arrest them. But things don't go to plan, and Liberty finds herself left in the desert to die. Fortunately, rescue comes in the unlikely shape of a young girl named Clementina, on the run herself — from a stepmother who happens to be the matriarch of the Wallace gang . . .